Rise of the Rattler

...m Walker lives with his family in Kent,
...e runs a design consultancy from an office
... the grounds of a beautiful country club.
... *of the Rattler* follows *Shipley Manor* and *The*
...lying Fizzler – also published by Faber – to
complete The Fizzle Trilogy.

Praise for *Shipley Manor*:

'This is a lively read, with more than enough
fantastical inventions and thrilling cliffhangers to
keep children turning the pages; just don't expect
impressionable readers ever to settle for a proper
job in future.' *Financial Times*

'An impressively fluent debut, with colourful,
larger-than-life characters – very good read aloud
material.' *Times Educational Supplement*

'An action-packed fantasy adventure story that
should appeal to fans of Roald Dahl . . . Filled with
humour, invention and larger-than-life characters.'
Bertrams Books

A RISE OF THE RATTLER

TIM WALKER

ff

faber and faber

First published in 2009
by Faber and Faber Limited
Bloomsbury House, 74–77 Great Russell Street,
London WC1B 3DA

Typeset by Faber and Faber
Printed in England by
CPI BookMarque, Croydon

A CIP record for this book
is available from the British Library

ISBN 978–0–571–23300–7

DISCLAIMER: Any resemblance between the people
in this book and any real person, living or
dead, is entirely accidental

2 4 6 8 10 9 7 5 3 1

In memory of Barbara du Preez

Polly opened her eyes. There was someone in her cabin.

Too scared to turn around, she lay still. Behind her in the darkness a drawer slid open.

There's nothing worth stealing in there, she thought, just socks and pants and those four peculiar pebbles I found on the roof. Please go away, whoever you are.

She heard the drawer close again, then waited for the search to continue.

But all she could hear was the hypnotic tick ... tick ... tick of her bedside clock, suggesting that, perhaps, no one was there after all, and that she could close her eyes again. So, as the seconds tick ... tick ... ticked into minutes, Polly drifted back to sleep, and her midnight visitor crept, finally, out of the room.

A Knock at the Door

Polly had always loved collecting pebbles. Often she would spend hours scouring the seashore, her eyes glued to the ground in search of the perfect stone, the *One* pebble that was rounder, or smoother, or more colourful than the rest, or that had the fossilised imprint of some long-dead sea creature embedded in it, or a recognisable shape tattooed on its marbled skin – a sea horse perhaps, or a P for Polly. She knew that she was unlikely ever to find the *One*, but that didn't matter. The fun was in the looking.

And then, suddenly, she had found four.

She had been on the roof of Shipley Manor. The volcano on Dollar Island had been ripped apart by the Fizzle the day before, filling the sky with flying debris. A few fragments had landed on the roof and she had gone up there to see what she could find. As she expected, most of them were sharp and jagged, not her favourites at all. But four of them were different. Special. At first sight the small, oval pebbles – one white, one blue, one grey and one black – appeared to be quite ordinary, their surfaces plain except for a faint, cloth-like graininess. But when Polly held them in her hand they felt warm and tingly against her skin, quite unlike anything she had ever picked up on the beach. She raced back downstairs, her newly found pebbles rattling in her pocket, and it was there, in the dimness of her cabin, that she discovered the strangest thing of all. She found that if she stared at any of the pebbles for long enough without blinking, she could see a tiny speck of light in its centre, pulsating like a spark of lightning in the heart of a dark storm cloud. Soon her eyes had begun to water and the specks were gone, but she had seen enough to know that the pebbles were special – even magical – and so she had put them in her top drawer for safe keeping.

Six months had passed since Shipley Manor and its crew had returned from the Caribbean. The pebbles had been stolen from Polly's cabin during their first night back in port, and even though some of her shipmates thought she must have imagined the incident, Polly had no such doubts.

'I know the pebbles were in the drawer when I went to sleep,' she was telling Tom, 'and I know they weren't there when I woke up. What more proof do you need?'

She and Tom were walking down the driveway on the Shipley Estate, having collected a copy of the *Shipley Gazette* from the postbox at the top.

'But why would anyone want to steal four pebbles, Polly? That doesn't make sense.'

He paused for a moment.

'Unless they were *magic* pebbles, of course.'

Polly rewarded his mockery with a playful prod of her Fizzlestick.

'Even if they weren't,' she replied 'they were definitely –'

'Enchanted?' Tom suggested, this time from a safer distance.

'Special!' she persisted. 'As though they were almost . . . alive. I don't care what anyone thinks. One day, I'll find out who stole them and get them back. You'll see.'

They continued on in silence, leaving dark, slushy footprints in the thin coating of winter snow which lay like white tissue over the driveway. As they rounded the last bend Tom remembered the first time that he had seen Shipley Manor – sitting majestically in its grounds bathed in sunlight – and

4

been stopped in his tracks by its grandeur. The old building was no longer there, of course. Having been swept down to the sea on a wave of Fizzle to become the world's first floating country house, it now lay in dock, shipshape and seaworthy, awaiting its next voyage. In its place, scattered randomly over the estate like breadcrumbs flung on to a lawn, was a higgledy-piggledy collection of sheds, caravans and portakabins. Tom winced at the sight, as he always did. Would it have hurt to arrange them in neat rows, he wondered – perhaps even numbered like the houses in a street? Instead, each one had been given a name like 'The-shed-by-the-old-tree-stump', and 'The-dented-caravan-facing-the-wrong-way' and 'The-green-portakabin-with-only one-window'. He felt an overwhelming urge to straighten them all up, just as he would any picture at home that looked even slightly crooked.

But at least he knew the untidiness was temporary. The Captain had plans to replace the makeshift camp with a magnificent new building – a school – to be known as the Shipley Manor Academy. When built it would be large enough to accommodate and teach a hundred or so of the children which he and his crew had rescued from Dollar Island, where they had worked like slaves in Sherman H. Kruud's bottling factory hidden deep within the volcano. Kruud and his associates had all been inside the volcano when it had erupted, attempting to breathe in the Fizzle gas to become Fizzlers. Whilst they'd had no desire to feel part of one enormous, worldwide family by drinking the magic water – Getting the Fizzle, as it was called – they had hoped that by breathing in its special gas they would acquire the same powers as Polly and Tom to read, and even enter, other people's minds. By visiting each other's minds – much like they might visit each other's houses – they would exchange their skills and talents as easily as neighbours sharing their garden tools, so that each would soon possess an almost superhuman range of abilities. Then, like burglars in the night they planned to steal the hard-earned skills of other Fizzlers, like Hopper Hawkins, to become invincible. Instead, perched on top of the Fizzle filter which Kruud had built especially for the purpose, they had become trapped, unable to escape. But all the children had been saved. Some had returned to their families in South America whilst others, like Pepe and Paco, had been found new homes in Jamaica. But many remained with nowhere to go, so the Captain had brought them to Shipley.

The townsfolk had rallied round immediately, donating dozens of temporary buildings – everything from old caravans to garden sheds –

which now covered much of the estate and acted as temporary classrooms and dormitories. Many of them were clustered around the estate's newest feature – a small lake – which had been created by diverting water from a nearby river into the hole where once Shipley Manor had stood. Among them, parked close to the water's edge, was a rather tired-looking double-decker bus. Polly called it the Slugbus, partly because its colour – a sort of dull, sluggy green – reminded her of a slug, but mostly because, in her opinion, it didn't travel much faster than one. The people of Shipley had presented it to the Captain so that he could take the children out and about. But apart from one or two trips to the docks to inspect Shipley Manor, there always seemed to be too much work on the estate to venture far beyond it. With winter approaching Polly had given up designing her own costumes and instead, assisted by Carlos – an eager, dark-haired boy who shared her passion for fashion – had spent all her time making outfits for them. Slugbucket and Moolah – formerly Kruud's most feared bamboo-master – had been equally busy, working round the clock with an army of helpers to extend the vegetable patches and orchards in order to feed all the extra mouths. They had even reinstated the slugpit, so that soon Shipley Manor's new residents were busy collecting slugs from the vegetable patches to fill it. Some, having spent years half-starved under Kruud's cruel regime, had to be reminded not to eat them, but they were fast learners and soon the slugpit was full again, oozing its nutritious slug juice back into the soil from holes in the bottom.

At the same time, to provide light and heat for the new community, Seymour and the Captain had spent every spare minute supervising the installation of a dozen wind turbines, which now stretched across the estate like a row of giant white daffodils, staring down the valley to the sea. And, of course, there were always children to look after, meals to cook, clothes to wash and lessons to teach – making day trips, even into town, a rarity. So, the Captain had converted the top deck of the Slugbus into a small café, which quickly had become the most popular meeting place on the estate.

As it turned out, there was no need to travel into town anyway because, for the past six months, the town had come to them. From the day of the children's arrival, volunteers had flooded through the gates, keen to contribute all kinds of help and support. The Captain couldn't say for sure whether their generosity and team spirit was a direct result of everyone Getting the Fizzle on Fizzle Friday – the day on which the Fizzle had fallen as rain into a billion waiting mouths. But either way he was grateful for it, even if, for some reason, the flow of volunteers had dwindled recently so that now Tom – who attended classes there – and his father Roger were the only regular visitors. Perhaps it was the weather, the Captain thought, even though he could remember winters being far colder when he was a boy, with snow often knee-deep covering the estate.

When they reached the bus Tom pushed open the folding door, and he and Polly ran up the steps, drawn by the smell of home cooking wafting down from the café. Upstairs, in the small kitchen area at the front of the bus, Polly's mother Maggie and the Captain were busy taking freshly baked cakes out of the oven whilst Calypso, her baby sister, sat in her high chair clapping her hands in anticipation.

'Perfect timing,' boomed the Captain, his chef's hat tickling the ceiling as he carried a chocolate cake over to the table. 'Moolah's taken the children for a run around the estate – we've just enough time for a slice of this before they fly up here and gobble the lot. And you've brought me the *Gazette* as well – how splendid! Perhaps I'll have time to read it for once.'

Polly handed him the newspaper.

'What's a Dry-Mouth?' she asked, taking a seat next to Tom. 'The newspaper says Mr Grub's one.'

The Captain squinted at the front page.

'Grub released from Shipley Prison,' the headline announced.

He frowned briefly at Grub's round, sweaty face which appeared below it, then plucked his reading glasses from his beard and began to read.

'From what I can tell, Polly,' he said, finally, 'a Dry-Mouth is someone who didn't taste the Fizzle when it rained down on Fizzle Friday. I suppose there must have been millions of people who didn't Get the Fizzle that day – people who were too old or too sick to go outside, miners working underground, airline pilots and their passengers thousands of feet up in the air –'

'– and prisoners in their cells,' asked Polly, 'like Mr Grub?'

'That's right, Polly, although I don't think it's very nice to call people names like that, even him.'

Maggie snorted from the kitchen, where she had begun baking bread.

'He and that . . . Venetia Pike . . . tried to steal everything we had, including the children. I think we're entitled to call him whatever we want.'

'Do you think he'll try again?' Polly asked, nervously.

The Captain shook his head.

'I'm sure he won't, Polly. According to the *Gazette* he spent his entire time in prison staring at a crumpled old photograph of his beloved Venetia

Pike, mumbling her name over and over again. Obviously the poor chap's quite harmless now.'

'At least we know he couldn't have stolen your pebbles all those months ago,' Tom observed.

'Either way, he'd better not show his face here again,' said Maggie, pummelling a lump of dough with her fist.

Just then there was a knock at the bus door.

A Bad Day Out

Captain Shipley answered the door. The visitor was dressed in a plain black business suit beneath which, in extravagant contrast, he wore a dazzling blue high-necked tunic. His short grey beard was trimmed neatly to a point, directing the Captain's gaze to the clear crystal pendant – shaped like a water droplet – which hung around the man's neck at the end of a long gold chain. Were it not for the man's eyes staring out, like white billiard balls, from behind his extra-thick glasses, the Captain might not have recognised him. But they, and the collection of biros lined up in his breast pocket like soldiers awaiting inspection, were unmistakable.

'Mr Tutt. How marvellous to see you.'

As a council inspector Mr Tutt had once been a regular visitor to Shipley Manor, responsible for ensuring that the premises complied with all the

Council's rules and regulations. The Captain stepped forward to shake his hand.

'I see you've come armed with your clipboard. Aren't you rather early to inspect our new school building? We haven't built it yet.'

Mr Tutt smiled and shook his head.

'I'm no longer the Council's buildings inspector, Captain Shipley. I serve a higher authority now.'

'A higher authority than Shipley Town Council?' the Captain joked. 'Surely there's no such thing!'

Mr Tutt didn't smile this time.

'Indeed there is, Captain. I work for His Effervescence the Grand Fizzler – with the Council's full support, of course.'

He touched the pendant reverently as he spoke his name. 'I'm here to investigate a rumour that you have several unregistered Dry-Mouths living on the estate.'

The Captain laughed, then fell silent as he realised that Mr Tutt wasn't joking.

'Do you mean children who didn't Get the Fizzle?'

'Correct, Captain. Some of the townspeople who worked here a few months ago learned that, whilst most of the children were on the roof of Shipley Manor when the Fizzle fell, several were not.' He handed a list of names to the Captain.

'That's right,' admitted the Captain, glancing at

the paper. 'Carlos and a few of the others were curled up in bed feeling seasick. Does it matter?'

'I'm afraid it does, Captain. The Grand Fizzler –' Mr Tutt touched his pendant again. '– has urged vigilance. As you know, Getting the Fizzle made each one of us feel connected to everyone else, which is why the people of Shipley so readily helped you establish this new community. But, as His Effervescence so wisely observes, whilst we may feel connected to *them* –' He paused; words of wisdom should never be rushed, after all. '– Dry-Mouths may not feel equally connected to *us*. Until they do, dare we trust them as much as we might trust each other? Are they not more likely than us to commit crimes and acts of selfishness against the community? And if so, should we really allow them to roam among us unidentified? The Grand Fizzler doesn't think so. And neither does Shipley Town Council.'

'Suffering seafrogs! So that's why you want these children to register, is it?' the Captain asked sharply. 'So that if something bad happens in Shipley, you'll know who to blame?'

Mr Tutt shrugged.

'I wouldn't put it quite like that, Captain, but let's face it, they're not quite . . . the same as us now, are they? The Grand Fizzler assures us that he is searching for a new source of Fizzle. But until its location is revealed to him all we can do is register those to whom it will eventually be given – albeit with a slight administration charge – and continue to send him donations so that he can carry on the search. As I'm sure you will, Captain.'

'Donations! I don't even know who this Grand Fizzler is!'

Now it was Mr Tutt's turn to look shocked.

'Really? Then perhaps you should read this, Captain,' he suggested. He pressed a small book into the Captain's hand. 'It's my own personal copy but you're welcome to borrow it. Perhaps you could drop it back at the Council offices when you register the children.'

'Do we have to register them?' the Captain asked.

'Not yet, but soon it will be compulsory. And, of course, the Council won't assist you in building a new school here until you do.' Mr Tutt turned to leave. 'Good day, Captain Shipley.'

That night, in the 'caravan-painted-with-sunflowers-behind-the-greenhouses', which he shared with Maggie, Polly and Calypso, the Captain pulled a small torch from his beard. Then, whilst the others slept, he began to study Mr Tutt's book. The front cover was plain except for a water droplet printed on it in clear, glossy varnish that made it look wet. Below it was the book's title: *Following the Fizzle*. The Captain turned to the first page and was greeted by a photograph of the author. Smiling wisely, the self-appointed Grand Fizzler was a frail, elderly man dressed in a blue silk robe made, it appeared, from the same shimmery fabric as Mr Tutt's tunic. A pair of watery blue eyes peered through his shoulder-length grey hair, whilst his beard – almost as long as the Captain's – tapered to a point in dozens of thin, silvery strands, each threaded with glass beads. A crystal pendant, similar to that worn by Mr Tutt only larger, was draped around his neck, his hand cradled beneath it as though he might be catching it as it fell. But it was the object that the man held like a shepherd's staff at his side which most astonished the Captain – a Fizzlestick, identical to Polly's in every way except that it appeared to be made out of gold. He knew that Polly had never met the Grand Fizzler, so how did he know about her Fizzlestick? And why would he want to carry one?

The Captain shook his head, mystified, and read on. The Grand Fizzler, or so he claimed, had been chosen by the Fizzle to speak on its behalf. He had been given a unique connection to it, he said, allowing him to gather and distribute its wisdom fluently in every major language. Clearly this was a feat which no ordinary man or woman could accomplish – only him, the Grand Fizzler.

Much of the book was concerned with praising the Fizzle for bringing people together on Fizzle Friday, and demanding contributions so that more of it could be found to complete the task. Sending money, the Grand Fizzler explained, was an expression of faith in the Fizzle and, one day soon, it would reward the world by falling again, or revealing its whereabouts to him. Until then, Dry-Mouths would be a constant threat to the community. So, be vigilant.

Unlike any other book the Captain had read, *Following the Fizzle* contained numerous advertisements. If you've Got the Fizzle, the book stated, then you have a duty to display it. All manner of clothes and trinkets were on offer, such as Mr Tutt's crystal pendant – which, the Captain discovered, was also available in a deluxe version with, it was claimed, a tiny bubble of Fizzle gas encased in its centre. He could also purchase a Fizzle certificate stating that he had, indeed, Got the Fizzle. Bearing the Grand Fizzler's signature alongside a special 'watermark', it would prove to any employer or customer that he was trustworthy. As far as the Captain could tell, no proof was required in order to obtain one, just a great deal of money. No wonder his Fizzlestick is gold, he thought.

He was also told that 'until the Fizzle returns no water shall be drunk on a Friday'. The Fizzle fell on a Friday, the Grand Fizzler reminded him, so that to drink ordinary water on the same day would, clearly, be an insult to it. Instead, a range of suitable alternatives were advertised, including, to the Captain's surprise, Kruud Kola. And so it went on until, as dawn broke, he closed the book.

'What I don't understand,' he whispered to Calypso, who was still asleep in her cot next to him, 'is how everyone's fallen for this poppycock.'

But he intended to find out. After breakfast he stowed away all the loose crockery at the top of the bus and started the engine. A day trip into town was long overdue anyway. Polly, Moolah and a dozen of the younger children, including Carlos, piled excitedly on to the Slugbus and they set off. Fifteen minutes later the Captain parked the bus in town, then led the way as they snaked up the High Street. Polly marched proudly alongside him with her Fizzlestick, whilst Moolah watched over the children from the tail end of the line. To most of them, having never seen Shipley before, the town might have looked normal. But to Polly and the Captain the change was obvious. The town was a sea of blue. Waves of shoppers – many dressed from head to toe in blue robes – flowed in and out of the shops, many of which had been painted blue to match the Grand Fizzler's costume. Outside, posters bearing His Effervescence's smiling face and the question 'Have YOU Got the Fizzle?' covered every wall and bus shelter. In the window of the electrical store the same smile shone out from a dozen television sets, from which, speaking Russian, Punjabi and Chinese as well as English, the Grand Fizzler urged vigilance against the Dry-Mouths and appealed for donations. In many of the shops – most of which displayed certificates assuring shoppers that 'We've Got the Fizzle' – there was a selection of Fizzle goods to buy as well as further opportunities to donate money. But despite the crowds, a few shops were empty of customers. The nearest was the florist shop owned by Mrs Bloom and her husband Bernard, who had often bought surplus flowers from the Shipley Estate. The Captain led his party inside.

'Don't tell me everyone's growing their own these days, Mrs Bloom,' he said, cheerily.

She looked up from behind the counter and shook her head.

'Haven't you heard, Captain Shipley? We're Dry-Mouths now. Bernard and I were stuck inside a plane heading off on our holidays when the Fizzle fell. So we didn't Get the Fizzle. There's no use pretending we did either. Bernard had told half of Shipley when we were flying so everyone knew where we were on Fizzle Friday. We've hardly sold any flowers since. Even when we do, I can see customers counting the stems when they leave the shop in case we've fiddled them. The same thing's happened to old Harry in the hardware shop. He was stuck in a hospital bed recovering from his hip operation on that day. Now he can't sell so much as a bag of nails, even though everyone *knows* he always added a few extra for luck.'

'Are you the only ones?' the Captain asked.

'Oh no,' replied Mrs Bloom. 'There are children in the school who flew off on holiday that day, too. Now, whenever so much as a pencil goes missing the other kids accuse them of stealing it, and even the teachers are suggesting that they're more likely to cheat in tests. So, now they're talking about herding them together into one classroom to keep an eye on them. The next thing you know they'll be sending them to special schools.'

She stared out of the shop window, shaking her head.

'I don't know what the world's coming to, Captain, really I don't. Everyone forgot their differences and got on so well for the first couple of months. Better than ever before. Then this Grand Fizzler character began setting people against each other. And now you can't escape him. He's everywhere, like a blue poison flowing through the town's veins.' She sighed. 'So . . . what kind of flowers would you like, Captain?'

'Anything that's not blue,' he joked.

'Roses?'

'Perfect. The redder the better. I'll have an armful please, Mrs Bloom . . . On second thoughts, make that two.'

A few minutes later the Captain left the florists hidden behind two huge bunches of roses. As they headed back towards the bus they walked past a bench. Sitting on it was a short, squat man with a thin moustache balanced like a wax crayon over his wet, rubbery lips. He was dressed in a long, tatty overcoat, with dandruff speckling his hunched shoulders like flecks of snow. Oblivious to the shoppers passing him by at a safe distance, he was staring sadly at a battered old photograph, mumbling to himself. The Captain failed to notice him, but Polly looked over her shoulder at the man as they passed. He looked so miserable, so dishevelled and lonely that, without thinking, she plucked a rose from the Captain's arms and ran back. The man looked up at the girl standing, slightly nervously, in front of him. He didn't seem to recognise her. But she recognised him. Mr Grub. She held out the rose, smiling, any anger she might still have felt for him having turned instantly to pity. He took it silently, then leant forward to watch her as she ran back to the Captain.

An hour later, the Captain loaded up the bus with shopping and waited as Moolah ushered the last straggler on board. He said goodbye to Polly – who had arranged to spend the afternoon in town with Tom – then slowly set off down the High Street towards Shipley Estate. The Captain smiled at the lively chit-chat coming from the children behind him, excited by their first day trip into Shipley. Then, suddenly, he overheard something which made his heart sink to his boots.

'Carlos can't sit with us,' one of the children declared loudly. 'He's a Dry-Mouth!'

The Captain pressed his foot against the brake and the bus screeched to a halt. He stared out of the window, fists clenched tight around the steering wheel, his eyes wide with anger. Outside, from a poster stuck to the wall of the Council offices, the Grand Fizzler stared back at him, his finger pointing accusingly as he demanded to know, 'Where were YOU when it rained on Fizzle Friday?' The Captain leaped down from the driver's cabin and strode, crimson faced, across the pavement. Then, watched by a small group of bemused blue-clad onlookers, he ripped the poster off the wall, screwed it up into a tight ball and stuffed it as deep as he could into the nearest bin.

'Minding my own damn business,' he growled. Next, he stuffed Mr Tutt's book into the Council letterbox and called up to the offices above, 'And if you think I'm about to register *any* of those children, you're mistaken.'

Finally, he jumped back into the bus and he and his passengers continued on their way in silence.

At the other end of the High Street, Polly looked up at the town clock. Tom was always on time so she knew that she had exactly five minutes to wait before he arrived. She crossed the road to the bus shelter where they had agreed to meet. Among the dozen or so people gathered there, there was a small, curly-haired boy waiting in line with his mother. He turned to Polly.

'You're not supposed to have one of those,' he said.

'One of what?'

'One of *those*,' he repeated, pointing to her Fizzlestick.

'Says who?' she replied.

'Says the Grand Fizzler, of course,' the boy told her. 'Only he's allowed to carry one. Everyone knows that.'

'That's silly,' Polly replied. 'I invented it!'

'Liar,' said the boy.

'I'm not lying. I made it to hook Fizzlefish out of the moat at home. I bet he doesn't even have a moat, let alone any Fizzlefish.'

A tall, thin man wearing blue robes and a carefully tapered ginger beard stepped out of the bus queue and marched up to her.

'Are you saying that His Effervescence the Grand Fizzler stole your idea?' he said, angrily. 'Are you calling him a thief?'

Polly shrugged, and looked nervously up at the clock. Two minutes to go. Why couldn't Tom be early for once?

'Perhaps you should give that to me,' the man continued. 'I think we should hand it in to the Council, don't you?'

But Polly didn't think that at all. Instead, she tightened her grip on the Fizzlestick and backed away. Suddenly the man lunged forward and grabbed it with both hands. He tried to pull it from her, but she clung on.

'Let go!' she screamed. *'Let go!'*

Then, as the clock began to strike, Tom came running to her aid.

'Leave her alone!'

He stepped in front of Polly and pushed the man

back. As the man's grip loosened he let go of the Fizzlestick and Polly went flying backwards with it clasped to her chest. She landed on her back, banging her head on the pavement with a sickening thud.

'Polly!' Tom squatted down beside her. 'Are you all right?'

'Fizzlesticks!' she said, sitting up to rub her head.

'Did you hear that, Mum?' said the boy. 'She swore!'

'Fizzlesticks isn't swearing!' Polly snapped back, as Tom helped her to her feet. He put his arm around her shoulder and tried to lead her away. But the circle of disapproving faces showed no sign of letting them pass. They were trapped.

'I think she must be a Dry-Mouth,' a woman whispered loudly to her neighbour. 'She called the Grand Fizzler a thief.'

The crowd murmured its disapproval. Emboldened by their support, the man stepped forward again, intent on retrieving the offending Fizzlestick, which this girl clearly had no right to possess. This time several onlookers stepped forward with him. He looked down at Polly sternly, then held out his hands.

'Give it to me,' he said.

'It's official,' the Captain told Maggie, stepping back inside their caravan. 'The world's gone stark raving bonkers.'

He tipped the contents of two carrier bags on to the bed, before sitting down next to Calypso's cot. Maggie handed him a mug of calming herbal tea, then began sifting through the various things which he'd brought back to show her: a signed photograph of the Grand Fizzler himself, sitting cross-legged in all his Fizzle finery surrounded by Fizzle bubbles; a Grand Fizzler doll that pretended to cry real Fizzle tears; a tiny packet of sand said to come from Dollar Island, the first place from which the Fizzle had erupted on Fizzle Friday.

'The town is suffocating under all this tat,' he told her, loosening his collar. 'And as for this –'

He handed her a copy of the official Shipley *Visitor's Guide*. As always, every shop in the town was listed. But in the latest version water droplets had been printed alongside all those which had Got the Fizzle and so been 'approved' by the Council. These were the ones to trust. Those without the symbol – for which there was also a hefty 'administration charge' – could expect few customers.

'Poor Mrs Bloom,' he said, shaking his head. 'This troublemaker is using the Fizzle to split Shipley and every other town in two, which is the exact opposite of what it was supposed to do. I watched the television news whilst I was in town. The same thing's happening all over the world. It doesn't matter who you are, where you're from or what you're like, the only thing anyone wants to know about you is whether you've Got the Fizzle or not. Even members of the same family are falling out because one of them didn't. This Grand Fizzler, or whatever he calls himself, is poisoning everything. What's more, he appears to have almost unlimited resources to keep forcing these crazy ideas on everyone, so who knows where it will all end? I should have realised what was happening. We have to do something, Maggie.'

She topped up his mug and noticed that his hand was trembling. She had never seen him so angry.

'The worst thing is,' he said, taking a deep breath, 'I've seen him speaking in so many languages that we have to take his claim about having special powers seriously. If he's breathed in the Fizzle gas like Polly and Tom he might be able to sneak into their minds – like that dreadful Venetia Pike sneaked into Polly's and interfered with her thoughts. We have to warn them as soon as they get back from town. Perhaps I should keep a lookout for them – I could do with some fresh air.'

With that he stood up and took his mug outside. He leant back against the caravan door, tipping his head back to fill his lungs before turning his gaze towards the driveway. Suddenly, there was Tom, striding down the pitted tarmac with Polly's Fizzlestick tucked under his arm. Walking knees bent beside him was a short, stocky man, wearing a rose in the lapel of his overcoat. He appeared to be carrying a bundle in his arms.

It was Polly.

Scarlett Changes Course

Scarlett Hawkins pulled off one of her fur-lined gloves and reached into the pocket of her battered old flying jacket. Like the jacket's previous owner – her great-grandfather, Hopper Hawkins – she never flew anywhere without an ample supply of toffees. She popped one into her mouth then, chewing slowly, checked the map spread out beside her on the co-pilot's seat. A thousand feet below, a vast expanse of Arctic whiteness stretched in every direction, so flat and featureless that only the drone of the plane's engine gave any sense that it was moving.

She looked at her watch. In half an hour she would reach the coast and her task of spotting new icebergs would begin. In some ways the work wasn't that different from her great-grandfather's job during World War One, she thought. Except, of course, that no one was shooting at her. Like Hopper, her mission was to fly out on patrol and record the movement of enemy troops. In this case the enemy was global warming – its troops the gigantic, jagged icebergs which it sent crashing into the ocean from melting glaciers to threaten shipping. But their danger was twofold. In time the icebergs would melt too, causing sea levels to rise up and attack the world's coastal defences with ever-increasing ferocity. This was a different kind of war, but a war none the less – against a common foe which, Scarlett knew, could be defeated only if the world forgot its differences and worked together.

For a while after Fizzle Friday that's what had happened, and Hopper Hawkins – his lifelong mission complete – died with a smile on his face. But since then a traitor had emerged in their midst. Cunningly disguised as a friend, he had sown seeds of division and unrest around the world and, in so doing, diverted the attention of its people from the real dangers facing them. And he called himself . . . the Grand Fizzler.

Unlike the Captain, Scarlett had watched – with increasing alarm – his influence grow from his first television broadcast. She had tried to discover who he was and where he came from, but he covered his tracks well. No one knew his real name and he appeared only rarely in public, staying long enough to make a few short pronouncements before being ushered away by a handful of young, blue-clad followers. Only one thing about him was clear to Scarlett, which was that he was destroying everything her great-grandfather had worked for. She had vowed to unmask him, to reveal his motive as the hunger for wealth and power that it most surely was. So far her investigations had drawn a blank, but she would keep trying. And in the meantime she would do the next best thing – she would look for more Fizzle and, at the same time, try to discover where it came from . . . and why.

She would begin her search in the Arctic, working as a pilot in one of the few places on earth where Hopper hadn't looked for the Fizzle already.

'Far too cold, even for an Englishman,' he had told her when she was about Polly's age. But there was one location where he thought it might be found, a place below which several fractures in the earth's crust – like those under the lake in which he'd first discovered it – converged like the spokes of a bicycle wheel.

'If you're ever in the Arctic, find the Big O,' was all he would say, shaking his head gleefully each time she suggested what the O might represent.

'No, it isn't an Owl, Scarlett,' he would tell her, 'not even a snowy one. And an orang-utan wouldn't set foot in the Arctic, would it? There aren't any jungles for it to swing around in. Keep guessing.' And she had. Ever since.

As the coastline came into view Scarlett glanced again at the map, drawing her fingertip north along the section of coast that she was due to patrol. Then she stopped. On the map, a few inches in the opposite direction, a ring of mountains was marked which formed a circle. At first she mistook it for a stain, perhaps left by the bottom of a damp coffee mug. But then the ring reminded her of something else . . . a Big O. No lake was indicated on the map, but she knew that the area hadn't been surveyed for many years. There was only one way to find out whether Hopper had been right. Scarlett looked at her watch. She had just enough time to fly over the area before returning to complete her patrol. So, she dipped her wing and the plane roared south. Half an hour later the mountains appeared on the horizon, then gradually filled the cockpit window as they grew closer, rising like a gaping mouthful of huge, jagged teeth. Scarlett swung inland and flew over the long white slope connecting them to the sea, aiming for a V-shaped gap between two of the tallest peaks. Then, suddenly, she was in the centre, rubbing her eyes in disbelief.

The area inside the ring of mountains was

almost a perfect circle. But where the land, or ice, should have been there was a hole, a mile across and a thousand feet deep, its perimeter wall rising in a single circular cliff face. She had to see what was inside. She took the plane down, circling lower and lower until she was below the level of the cliffs. At the bottom, a smooth surface of ice was beckoning her to land. She had no idea whether it would be thick enough to bear the weight of the plane. But she had to try. She continued to spiral downwards until, with a final turn, she landed the plane with a few bunny hops and brought it to rest close to the centre. She kept the engine running, peering out of the side window for any signs of cracking below, ready to take off again quickly. But the ice held. She pulled the ear flaps of Hopper's old flying hat down over her rust-red curls and stepped down on to the surface. Despite its thickness the ice was unusually smooth and clear, and she could see water moving slowly underneath it. She reached back into the plane and retrieved an ice saw – standard survival kit on board an ice patrol – then moved a short distance away to begin cutting.

The ice was unexpectedly hard, but after a few minutes she had cut a neat circular hole about a shoulder's width across. Satisfied, she looked up. Strangely, the plane appeared to be further away from her. There was no wind – she had checked. But there was no doubt it had moved. Slowly she stood up and made her way towards it, just as it began to slide faster and faster away from her. Then she realised. The lake wasn't flat. Instead, it sloped away gently – almost unnoticeably – from the centre towards its perimeter. As the plane accelerated towards the cliff face she tried to run after it. But her boots barely gripped the ice, causing her to slip and slide so that the plane remained just ahead of her grasp, edging further and further away. And then it was gone, pirouetting off into the distance like an Olympic skater, until it was little more than a dot. A few seconds later she heard the plane smash against the cliff wall and watched, numbly, as a huge ball of fire rolled up the cliff face like a giant orange flower, bursting into bloom at the end of a smoky black stem. The fireball burnt itself out halfway up, she noted. Nobody, except her, would have seen it. She craned her neck to the top of the cliff, then turned in a dizzying circle looking for some way out. But there was none that she could see. Unable to contain her anger any longer, she hurled the ice saw as far as she could across the ice. When she turned back to the hole, she found that she was no longer alone. Lolloping towards her from the other side, its teeth bared ready for combat, was a huge polar bear.

She had to think quickly. All that lay between her and the animal was the hole that she had cut with the ice saw. Her only chance was to reach it before the bear and hope that her great-grandfather had been right. If the lake was indeed full of Fizzle, perhaps it would find a way to save her. And if not, then at least she would stay alive for a couple of minutes longer. She began running towards the bear, as though she intended to meet it in combat. For a moment it stopped, rearing up on its hind legs to roar, claws and fangs bared as if to demonstrate in advance the full might that it was about to unleash against her. And then it dropped back on to its huge front paws and charged into battle.

Scarlett reached the hole a split second before it. She took a deep breath and jumped into the dark, icy water. The animal lunged after her but the gap was barely wide enough for its head. Instead, it thrust one of its front paws in after her and began scything long arcs through the water with its curved, razor-sharp claws. Suddenly, a claw pierced the cuff of Scarlett's flying jacket, catching her like a fish on the end of a hook. Luckily Hopper's jacket had always been a size too big for her, so she raised her arms and let it slip off over her head. Then she kicked hard, pushing herself below the ice until she was beyond the bear's deadly reach.

As the air began to escape from her mouth she rose to float face up under the ice, her lips almost kissing it as she sucked what air she could from the small gap between it and the water. 'Help,' she gasped, to no one in particular. The outside of her body was already numb with cold but, oddly, she could feel the warmth inside her spreading back into her fingers and toes. In her efforts to escape the animal's grasp she had barely noticed the billions of tiny bubbles which had begun clinging to her, cocooning her in a thin layer of Fizzle gas, holding the heat inside her like a thermos flask. Then she realised that a bubble the size of a diver's helmet had grown around her head, allowing her to breathe freely.

Hopper had been right. She had found the Fizzle. If, with its help, she could survive long enough, perhaps the bear would retreat and she could escape. But it showed no sign of giving up. Instead, baring its teeth through the ice just a foot above her face, it began trying to claw its way through to her, its hot, dripping saliva burning like acid into the icy surface. If only she could scare it off, or it could, somehow, be tempted away by the prospect of an easier meal elsewhere. As she wishfully imagined the polar bear being summoned by a distant dinner bell, so she felt the water around her begin to swirl. She rolled over to look down into the blackness, from which a circle of silver bubbles had begun to rise towards her. As they reached the surface, she saw what had created them. Seals. A dozen of them, arriving fat and succulent like the main course at a polar bear's banquet. Scarlett looked up through the ice. In a flurry of dancing paws the polar bear had begun to spin around like a dog chasing its tail, mesmerised by the extravagant gourmet feast circling just below it. Then she switched her gaze back to the seals, which had spread out, nose to tail, in a perfect circle around her. Suddenly, one of them tilted its head sideways and glanced at her. In that moment, like two best friends spotting each other across a crowded room, there was an instant connection between them, across which passed a silent message that was as clear as any spoken word. Get ready, the seal was telling her. Then it broke the circle, streaking off in a straight line towards the shore. As the others followed it so the polar bear lumbered dizzily after them, all thought of Scarlett having been spun out of its head.

This was her chance. Quickly, she spun around looking for the hole through which she had jumped, only to find nothing but solid ice above her. Now, she realised, that having twisted and turned out of the bear's reach she had become lost beneath a ceiling of ice large enough to cover a small town. She punched it in frustration. Her situation seemed hopeless. But her great-grandfather never would have given up. And neither would she. For as long as her Fizzle skin kept the cold at bay and she had enough strength to stay afloat, she would search for a way out. That's what he would have done. Briefly she closed her eyes to think of him, hoping to summon up some of the courage and determination that she remembered in him so well.

When she opened them a few seconds later, there he was – swimming through the water towards her.

A Close Shave

Maggie pressed the packet of frozen peas against the back of Polly's head. They were in the Slugbus Café, where the Captain had gathered everyone together for an emergency meeting.

'Noice lump, Polly – best ever, oi reckon,' said Slugbucket, squeezing on to the seat next to her.

She smiled, weakly.

'Thanks, Slugbucket.'

Apart from Seymour and Edna – who were away visiting Seymour's mother – all the shipmates were there. They listened, open-mouthed, as Tom described Polly's terrifying ordeal, and how Mr Grub – who was seated at the back of the bus, staring quietly out of the window – had stormed to her rescue. The circle of angry shoppers had closed around them like a noose, Tom said, and the man with the beard was about to confiscate Polly's

Fizzlestick. Then, suddenly, Mr Grub had burst through the crowd in his black coat, roaring and flapping his arms like an enormous crow, and scattered the shoppers in all directions. After that, Polly had said that she felt faint and wanted to come home, but none of the buses would stop for them. So, Mr Grub had carried her all the way back to the estate. Polly looked up at her mother.

'He doesn't have anywhere to live,' she said. 'Can he stay with us?'

Maggie glared suspiciously at Grub, her lips pressed tight together as though the mere thought of him staying was like sucking a raw lemon. Clearly she hadn't forgotten his past crimes, let alone forgiven them. And still he looked, and smelled, just as odious as she remembered him.

The Captain leant over to her.

'He's a Dry-Mouth *and* an ex-convict,' he whispered, not that she needed reminding. 'If we don't take him in, who will?'

'I'll look after him,' volunteered Moolah. Having been the only girl among Kruud's bamboo-masters – and hated for being faster, tougher and smarter than all the boys – she knew how it felt to be an outsider. 'Perhaps he could help Slugbucket and me in the vegetable patches – and there's a spare caravan next to mine. If I fix the roof he could sleep in that.'

The Captain caught Slugbucket's eye across the table.

'That's all right by me, Cap'n. Jus' as long as 'e pulls 'is weight.'

Then their eyes returned to Maggie.

She hesitated . . .

Then, she hesitated some more . . .

'Fine, he can stay,' she said eventually, raising a hand in surrender. 'Just make sure you keep an eye on him, that's all.'

The Captain clapped his hands together.

'Good. That's settled then. Now, let's get down to business.'

He retrieved a pair of carrier bags from under the table and tipped out the items which he'd bought in town. Then he went on to describe how the town had changed over the past months, and how the Grand Fizzler was using the Fizzle to set people against each other. He had no idea who the so-called Grand Fizzler was, or where he lived, he said, but clearly he had to be stopped from spreading his poison any further. And it was their job to stop him.

'We delivered the Fizzle to Dollar Island and started the whole thing off. We have to fix it. No one else will. The only trouble is that no one knows anything about him. But he must have been hugely rich to begin with, otherwise he wouldn't have been able to bombard the world with books and posters and dolls of himself, let alone take over entire radio and television channels to broadcast all this Dry-Mouth nonsense. What do you think, Moolah?'

She seemed distracted by the Grand Fizzler doll.

'All these things are made by the same company,' she said, peering at the tag attached to the doll's ankle. The Captain put on his reading glasses and took the doll from her. Then he checked the name printed on the packet of Dollar Island sand: *Made by KPRC Industries*.

'So they are . . . but how does that help us?'

'I'm not sure,' Moolah replied, 'but Mr Kruud's friends – the ones who arrived on Dollar Island just before the volcano exploded – were called Punjabootee, Robovich and Ching.'

'K, P, R, C!' said Polly.

'Jumping jellyfish, you're right,' said the Captain. 'Maybe those scoundrels aren't quite as dead as we thought.'

'But they was all trapped inside the volcano when it erupted,' Slugbucket reminded him. 'Polly locked 'em inside the Fizzle chamber an' that nasty Pike woman threw away the key. You saw 'er do it. They can't 'ave escaped. B'sides, every newspaper in the world says they disappeared that day. Ain't that roight, Polly?'

But Polly wasn't listening. Instead, she was hugging her knees, rocking back and forth on her seat, shivering uncontrollably.

'I'm c-c-cold,' she complained.

Maggie looked down at the packet of frozen peas, astonished at its effect, before realising that something else was causing Polly's teeth to chatter. Then, suddenly, as Polly glanced out of the frost-covered window she thought she saw a flash of white fangs on the other side of the glass.

'Aaaargh! A p-p-polar bear!' she shivered.

Maggie took off her cardigan and wrapped it tight around her daughter.

'There's no polar bear outside, Polly. You must have hit your head harder than we thought.'

'No, she d-d-didn't.'

They turned to see Tom shivering too, as though suddenly he'd fallen into an icy lake.

'I saw it as well – but it was in my head, as though I was seeing it through another person's eyes. I heard a v-v-voice too, just as sometimes I can hear Polly's even though we're miles apart. It was c-c-calling for help.'

'Do you know who it was?' the Captain asked.

Tom shook his head.

'Their voice was just a whisper, as though they d-d-didn't want to be overheard, or were t-t-too weak to call any louder.'

'P-p-polar bears live in the Arctic, don't they?' said Polly. 'That's where Scarlett said she was going – to patrol for icebergs and look for more F-f-fizzle. She must have found some and b-b-breathed in the gas. Otherwise, we wouldn't have been able to hear her.'

Tom nodded in agreement.

'I think we'd better find out,' said the Captain. He wrapped his jacket around Tom, then strode off to the bus with Moolah close behind. A few minutes later she returned loaded with blankets from one of the dormitories. Once wrapped snugly inside the borrowed bedding and with cups of hot chocolate pressed between their hands, Polly and Tom began to warm up. By the time the Captain returned, they had stopped shivering.

'I've just spoken to the Arctic Ice Patrol . . .' He paused. The news was bad. 'Scarlett's plane has gone missing.'

Polly jumped up.

'We have to go there!'

'I agree,' said the Captain. 'Even if they rescue her, she must have found more Fizzle. And if we know that, so will the Grand Fizzler. He's probably on his way there now in a private jet or something. Don't worry, Polly, we'll find Scarlett, and after that I'm going to dig this scoundrel out from whatever stone he's hiding under, and make him put a stop to all this Dry-Mouth lunacy.'

So that was settled. With over a hundred children living on the estate, all that remained was to decide who would accompany the Captain on the expedition, and who would stay to look after them. After some discussion it was agreed that Maggie and Calypso would remain behind, along with Seymour and Edna, who would ensure that no lessons were missed in the classrooms. Polly had insisted on going, of course, not least because she couldn't safely set foot in the town again until the Grand Fizzler had been unmasked, and people had returned to their senses.

Subject to his father's permission, Tom had volunteered to go, too. He and Polly had always been a team, after all, and as the proud possessor of Hopper Hawkins's flying skills he alone would be able to fly Scarlett's plane should the need arise. Besides, there were all the other special abilities that Hopper had given to him before he died. He had invited Tom into the basement room in his mind, in which his skills were stored inside a collection of sweet jars. Then, he had allowed him to eat whichever sweets he liked, so that he could absorb the abilities contained within them. In this way Tom had also become a superb climber, an accomplished skier and a trained parachutist, any of which might turn out to be useful. Moolah knew that she had to go too, especially if, somehow, Kruud and his associates were still alive and involved with the Grand Fizzler. No one knew Kruud's devious mind better than she, and if some of the other bamboo-masters were still working for him – well, she knew how to handle them, too. She glanced to the back of the bus where Mr Grub, with a slow and loving fingertip, had just finished writing 'Venetia' in the condensation on the inside of the window.

'He might slow you down if he comes with us,' the Captain warned her.

She grinned back at him, clicking her knuckles.

'Nothing slows me down,' she said.

Finally, all eyes turned to Slugbucket, who had remained silent. Although there was little to do in the garden during the winter, the makeshift classrooms regularly sprang leaks during bad weather and there was always plenty to do. And he knew that the Captain would prefer a strong pair of hands to remain, not least to protect the children on Mr Tutt's list from any threat posed by followers of the Grand Fizzler or, even, by some of the other, more impressionable youngsters on the estate. With an increasingly hostile atmosphere in town, he knew also that Maggie and the children would feel safer if he remained.

'Oi'll stay,' he said, at last. 'Oi'll enjoy chasin''

them townsfolk away if they decide to turn up wi'
their pitchforks an' flamin' torches.'

But Tom had a better idea. He turned to the
Captain.

'My father can stay here instead,' he suggested.
'He's always said that he'd be happy to live on the
estate for a few weeks if you needed him to.'

Slugbucket's eyes lit up.

'Well, I s'pose the garden could manage for a few
weeks without me . . . so long as yer 'appy about it,
Maggie?'

Maggie nodded, smiling.

'If Tom's father is anything like him, this place
will be shining like a new pin before you get back.'

And so it was settled. That night they would load
the bus with food and provisions whilst Tom
returned home to tell his father about the trip and
pack his rucksack. All being well, they would leave
for the docks in the morning.

The next day, Polly waited for Tom outside the bus.
She heard his father's car door slam, then a few
seconds later Tom came running down the
driveway, a bulging rucksack bouncing on his back.
His father followed, a pair of matching suitcases
rumbling on their wheels behind him.

'Dad's agreed,' he said, jumping aboard. 'He's

going to drop his bags in the spare caravan before coming to the docks to see us off.'

They could hear footsteps upstairs in the café.

'There's something we have to do before we go up there,' Polly whispered, dragging him on to a downstairs seat. 'If the Captain's right about the Grand Fizzler being able to enter other people's minds, we have to make sure he keeps out of ours.'

'How?' asked Tom.

'Easy,' replied Polly. 'We imagine that our minds are impenetrable fortresses. The walls won't stop us from hearing each other's thoughts, but if we want to visit each other's minds properly we'll have to use something that lets only us inside.'

'Like what?'

'Like a password,' she replied, taking out the velvet Jumblupp bag which she always carried. Inside it were dozens of small pebbles, each painted with a letter of the alphabet. Normally she used them to play Jumblupp, the word-inventing game that she had made up, but today she could put them to another use.

'I think we should let the Jumblupp letters decide what it is,' she told Tom. 'We'll take pebbles out of the bag one at a time and the first real word that we can make will be our password.'

Tom agreed, and soon there were five letters spread out on the seat between them.

'Got it,' whispered Polly, quickly shuffling them around. Tom nodded. No one would be able to enter their minds without the password, and no one could discover the password without entering their minds. Perfect.

Polly slid the pebbles back into the bag, then she and Tom bounded up the stairs. At the top she stopped. A strange man was holding her mother by the shoulders. His face was strong and angular with long, pointed sideburns leading down to a square jaw – smooth except for an inch-long purple scar on the side of his chin. Then she noticed that her mother was smiling at him, and stroking his cheek. Polly felt sick, as though the world she knew had suddenly turned upside down, inside out and back to front all at once. Why were they looking at each other so lovingly? The Captain would be heartbroken if he knew. Suddenly the stranger leaned forward to kiss her mother.

'Noooooo!'

Before Tom could stop her, Polly flew at the man, swinging her Fizzlestick at his shin. He moved back just in time to watch the stick crack the table leg in front of him.

'Blithering blowholes, hold your fire, Polly – it's me!'

Polly looked up.

'Captain?'

'Who else would it be? Now . . . tell me honestly,' he said, squatting down and lifting her hand to his face, 'do you think I look younger without my beard?'

Polly ran her fingers along his scar.

'Wow, was that made by a pirate's cutlass?' she asked, hoping to prompt one of the Captain's seafaring stories.

Instead, he winced, his pale cheeks reddening slightly.

'Actually . . . I cut myself shaving,' he confessed. 'On my first day at sea I happened to be below decks with a mirror in one hand, and a cut-throat razor in the other, when the ship was hit by a massive wave. After that I decided that seafaring and shaving didn't mix, so I haven't used a razor since. Until today, of course. If half of Shipley wants to grow a beard in honour of this so-called Grand Fizzler, then let them. But I won't be growing mine again until we've unmasked the scoundrel.'

He glanced down at the table on which Maggie had laid out the contents of his beard like bric-à-brac at a boot fair.

'Creeping crabsticks,' he said. 'I was sure I'd finished that sandwich. And my snow goggles, too. How marvellous – I've been looking for those for years.'

The journey to the docks was uneventful, the mood inside the bus thoughtful. As Slugbucket drove through the snow-flecked countryside, Polly and Tom listened quietly for any message from Scarlett, whilst the Captain planned their route and, occasionally, skipped down the stairs to double-check the provisions which filled most of the bottom deck. Mr Grub sat at the back, across the aisle from Moolah, on whose lap Nautipus was curled up asleep, purring quietly. But it was Seymour who was deepest in thought, his eyes flicking to the ceiling as the two halves of a puzzle began to slot together in his head. When they arrived at the docks the Captain strode across the drawbridge joining Shipley Manor to the quayside, and pushed open its heavy oak doors. Then, as Seymour swept past he followed him straight up into the Crow's Nest, pausing only to pat the stonework affectionately on his way through the house.

As always the Crow's Nest was in a mess. But it was no longer buried under Seymour's usual collection of scientific apparatus and half-built inventions. Instead, every surface was strewn with maps, plans, surveys and charts. Like Scarlett,

Seymour had wanted to solve one of the Fizzle's secrets – to discover where it came from, to find its home. For the past few months his researches had brought him to the Crow's Nest almost every weekend where, undisturbed, he had pored over hundreds of geological maps looking for clues. But Scarlett's disappearance had narrowed down the search . . . dramatically. By the time Polly and Tom arrived a few seconds later he was rummaging around for the two maps which, he was certain, would tell them where Scarlett could be found.

'Right, here's the first one,' he said, handing a large map to Polly. 'That shows the Arctic coastline. Would you mind laying it out over the desk, please, Polly?'

Immediately she obliged.

'Now, if Scarlett's gone off course she could be anywhere on that map. Finding her will be like looking for a needle in a haystack. But I don't think she will have stumbled on the Fizzle by accident, you see.' His head disappeared under the work-bench as he hunted through a pile of boxes. 'Somehow she'll have . . . worked out where it was. So, our best chance of finding her will be to find the Fizzle.' He lifted a box on to the workbench and tipped out its contents. 'These are all geological maps,' he explained, frantically flicking through them until he found the one he was looking for. 'This is it. Apart from the Arctic coastline it shows nothing but underground fault lines. I had them all printed on tracing paper so I could lay them over the top of each other. Tom, would you mind –?'

Tom took the map and unfolded it. At first glance there were so many fault lines that the map reminded Tom of a giant leaf skeleton but, on Seymour's advice, he found that if he half-closed his eyes most of these disappeared, leaving only the thicker, deeper fault lines visible. By contrast, these were straight and uniform, and met at a single point. He laid the map on top of Polly's so that the coastlines of the two merged.

'That's it!' said Seymour. 'Do you see where those fault lines meet – smack bang in the middle of those mountains?' He prodded the map emphatically with his finger. 'That's where I think you'll find Scarlett.'

Slugbucket arrived in the doorway.

'We're all packed, Cap'n. Jus' our goodbyes to say an' then we're ready ter go.'

Seymour turned to leave.

'Oh, one last thing,' he said, reaching for the plain canvas bag which hung from the back of his wheelchair. He removed two identical dark-blue boxes from inside, and handed one each to Polly and Tom. 'This is a bit of a joint effort,' he explained. 'Slugbucket thought of them, I made them and Maggie designed the boxes for them.'

Polly looked down at the beautiful package resting in her hands. The box was circular, about the same size as a small chocolate cake. The cardboard lid had been decorated beautifully, with an ornate gold star around which the four points of the compass had been inscribed. Stretching around the outside of the box in elegant, hand-drawn script were the words 'Self-Locating Unification Gyroscope'.

Polly's mouth dropped open.

'Oh, it's beau-u-utiful,' she said, turning the box around to read the inscription.

'They're to help you and Tom find each other if you become separated,' explained Seymour.

'But we can listen to each other's thoughts,' said Polly. 'I can just tell him where I am.'

'I know,' said Seymour, 'but perhaps the Grand Fizzler might be able to hear you, too. These will help you keep track of each other secretly.'

'You mean like a pair of . . . Magical Compasses?' asked Polly, eagerly.

Seymour hesitated. Perhaps Maggie had packaged their gifts a little too beautifully.

'Er, not quite . . . but they're just as useful,' he insisted. 'I call them Slug-o-meters for short.'

Polly lifted the lid. Inside, nestling amid folds of

purple velvet, was a plain matchbox. She pushed it open.

'It's a slug!'

Seymour blushed. The packaging had definitely been a mistake.

'That's right. But it's no ordinary slug,' he explained hastily. 'Do you remember those two slugs that breathed in the Fizzle gas so that they became connected with each other, even when they were on opposite sides of the house?'

'Oi'll never forget 'em, that's fer sure,' said Slugbucket. 'Oi 'ad to eat one o' them jus' to find out where Tom was.'

'That's what gave Slugbucket the idea for the Slug-o-meter,' Seymour explained. 'The other slug died of sluggy old age a few weeks ago, but luckily Slugbucket had one bottle of Fizzle left. So I poured it into the Fizzle Filter, popped our two slippery friends into the chamber on top and turned them both into super-slugs. Now, no matter how far apart they are, they each know where the other one is. All you have to do is place one of them on the palm of your hand and it will point automatically towards the other, no matter how far away it is.'

Polly hugged Slugbucket tight.

'I'll keep it safe, always,' she promised.

'Good,' he replied. ''Cause oi don't think I could face 'avin' ter eat another one.'

Polly and Tom slipped the matchboxes into their pockets, and they returned briefly to the drawbridge to say their farewells. The mood outside was heavy with concern for Scarlett. There were no brass bands, no bunting, no cheering crowds to see them off. Just promises of safe returns and warnings about frostbite and polar bears. Then the drawbridge was raised and the huge, churning paddle wheels began slowly to push Shipley Manor out of the docks. The Captain stood at the ship's wheel, grim but determined. Having alerted the Ice Patrol to Scarlett's suspected whereabouts, he knew that if the search planes couldn't find her, then it would be a full seven days before he and his crew could join the search, and there was no guarantee that they would find her in time. Even if they succeeded, he knew that far more than Scarlett's life was at stake. As if to remind him, the Grand Fizzler's face stared out accusingly from a huge new banner hanging from the end of the harbour wall, challenging every incoming visitor with the same question: 'Have you Got the Fizzle?' Instinctively, the Captain touched the hilt of his sword as he passed it. Then, as Shipley Manor headed out to sea, he set the paddle wheels to full power.

The Grand Hotel

Five days had passed since Shipley Manor set sail. At first, Polly had enjoyed being back in the house. Having spent most of her life there she had missed it, and for a while had been content to pass the time flying her home-made kite from the roof, or sitting at the familiar kitchen table watching the Captain's huge chef's hat wobbling as he chopped vegetables, or trying to break her own speed record for sliding down the helter-skelter from the Crow's Nest to the courtyard. But the days had begun to drag by, and as the air outside grew steadily colder she knew that Scarlett's life was in greater and greater peril with each passing hour – and that she could do nothing about it.

Except wait . . .

And wait . . .

And wait . . .

She strode into Tom's cabin and plonked herself cross-legged on the end of his bunk. He continued reading his book, wrapped in concentration.

'The Captain's just checked again with the Ice Patrol,' she told him. 'Scarlett still hasn't been found.'

She and Tom knew that already, of course, the low call for help having continued since they set sail. They had tried talking to Scarlett in the same way that they could talk to each other – silently, by listening to each other's thoughts. But either Scarlett didn't want to talk or she was too weak to, because the whisper in both their heads simply said, 'Help.' Perhaps she was frightened that the Grand Fizzler could overhear her, and she didn't want to give away her location to him.

'And we still have two days to go before we reach the coast,' Polly continued. 'Even if the sea stays calm.'

'Then we might be too late,' Tom replied, closing the book. 'I've been reading all about Arctic survival. If she's alive she must have found shelter, but after five days she'll have run out of survival rations. If she's injured and can't find food she'll be too weak to move, and then she won't be able to keep warm, and then . . .' He bit his lip, thoughtfully. 'We need help,' he said.

'From who? Every plane in the Ice Patrol is

searching for her already. Who else is there?'

'The Grand Fizzler,' he replied. 'If we saw the polar bear he will have seen it too, and worked out that Scarlett has become a Fizzler. There's a good chance that he's heading up there now to get his hands on the Fizzle, probably in something faster than a floating country house, too. He might even have arrived. We have to talk to him, and make sure he saves Scarlett before it's too late.'

'Then let's ask him.'

'I've tried,' said Tom. 'But he won't answer me. There's only one way to speak to him and that's by going into his mind, the same way that I went into Venetia Pike's.'

'I'll come too,' said Polly. 'You've told me how you mind-hop. I'll just close my eyes and count backwards and imagine that I'm flying over rooftops. Then I'll look for a house that reminds me of him.'

'You can't, Polly. It's too dangerous. Last time I was attacked by giant snakes and stung by a scorpion, remember?'

Polly folded her arms.

'Go on then,' she huffed. 'I'll keep a lookout.'

Tom hesitated. He was expecting more of a fuss.

'Well . . . are you going to do it or not?' she said.

Tom nodded, then lay back on the bunk with his arms aligned neatly at his sides, and closed his eyes. He began to count backwards from ten, imagining himself as a kite flying high from the hilltop overlooking Shipley. By the time he reached six he could feel the imaginary wind tugging at him. As he reached three he thought he felt Polly lie down next to him and take hold of his hand. But it was too late to stop her. Suddenly the real world in his cabin was gone and the wind was carrying him over the rooftops, with Polly flapping along beside him like a young bird on its first outing.

'Polly! You don't need to flap your arms like that. Just keep them level and let the wind take you,' he told her. 'You're wobbling all over the place.'

'What are we supposed to be looking for?' she shouted.

'Something "grand", I suppose . . . the sort of place where a Grand Fizzler might live,' replied Tom.

They continued to soar over the rooftops, their eyes and ears and noses on high alert for any sight or sound or smell that might remind them of him. Slowly Polly began to drift apart from Tom, drawn like a moth to a light flickering on the horizon.

Tom turned to follow her. Far ahead, perched high on a rooftop, a huge neon sign buzzed and crackled, imposing its hot, garish colours over the rows of modest houses which surrounded it. *The Grand Hotel* it blared. The building upon which it stood was easily the ugliest Polly and Tom had ever seen. The two bottom floors appeared to match the ordinary houses around it, but a huge hole had been knocked in the front wall to make way for a grand entrance, from which a dark blue rain canopy stretched across the pavement bearing the name of the hotel in gold letters along its sides. Above the first two storeys any resemblance to the houses surrounding it – or to any architectural good taste – ceased. From there, additional floors had been bolted on, growing ever wider into the sky, so that the entire building was top heavy. Each floor appeared to have been designed by a different architect determined to outdo the creator of the floor below, so that countless spires, domes, turrets and terraces sprouted from the building like an outbreak of warts.

'Yuk! How did they get planning permission for *that*?' gasped Polly as, at last, they lowered themselves to the ground in front of it. A man dressed in a doorman's tailcoat and top hat stood glumly by the entrance. At once his tortoise-like face seemed familiar. Tom realised that the last time they'd seen him the man had been wearing a chauffeur's hat and driving a long white limousine. He was Mr Kruud's butler.

'May we come in?' asked Tom.

Kruud's manservant touched the rim of his hat

and smiled, thinly.

'Why not, sir? Everyone else does,' he replied, ushering them through the revolving doors.

As they entered the hotel they could see that only the outer shell of the original house remained. The inside had been hollowed out to create a large open foyer befitting a 'grand' hotel. Here, various designers seemed to have competed against each other to impose their own brand of luxury on the interior, so that ornate gold cabinets and ancient Persian rugs fought for space with – much to Polly's disgust – hand-carved ivory coffee tables and leopard-skin sofas. At the far end of the room behind a well-polished reception desk stood another man, quivering slightly, like a character drawn with a shaky hand. Despite wearing a different uniform he looked identical to the doorman except that he was, unless Tom was imagining things, slightly smaller. Tom looked back outside to see if the doorman was still there.

'Yes, that's me, too,' the receptionist sighed. 'I'm the butler, the doorman, the receptionist, the lift boy – a man of many talents, you might say.'

'We're looking for the Grand Fizzler,' announced Polly. 'Is he here?'

The man's head shrank down into his collar, his tired, bloodshot eyes darting nervously left and right, as though he was sure that he was being watched. Then he nodded, quickly.

'Where is he? We need to talk to him. Urgently.'

'I can't say, miss. I'm under strict orders not to say anything about him. If I do . . . *they'll* know.'

'Who'll know?'

Again the man checked that no one was watching him.

'Them,' he whispered, jabbing his finger towards the ceiling.

'And they wouldn't be pleased,' he continued, tears welling up in his eyes. 'Oh no, they wouldn't be pleased *at all*. They'd make me forget something precious again – erase it from my memory. For ever. That's what happens when I do something wrong, you see, sir. Last week –' He paused to dab his eyes with a handkerchief. '– they made me forget every holiday I'd ever had. Each one was stored as a picture postcard in my memory, with photographs of all the wonderful places I'd visited on one side and my recollections written on the other. They took them outside and burned the lot. I could hear them laughing. I can't remember any of my holidays now. I might as well never have been on them. And all because I was late delivering Mr Kruud's milk and meringues.'

Polly gasped.

'Mr Kruud is *here*?'

The man nodded, weakly.

'I have no idea how it happened, sir. I remember I was on board Mr Kruud's yacht taking Arthur – that's his pet seal – for his yearly whisker trim. I was tidying up as usual when I found something that looked like a coffee-maker sitting on a table. There seemed to be nothing but water inside. I didn't drink any, of course – Mr Kruud has never allowed me to eat or drink any leftovers. So I took it to the galley to wash up. As soon as I removed the lid I smelt something slightly odd wafting up from the top.'

'Fizzle gas,' said Tom. 'That was a Fizzle Filter you were holding. Mr Kruud built a huge one inside the volcano so that he and his friends could breathe in the Fizzle gas. He must have made a model to test first.'

'Well, I got a whiff of whatever was inside it, sir – just before I heard the volcano explode in the distance. The next thing I knew, I could hear Mr Kruud barking orders at me. But he wasn't on the yacht. He was –' The man choked back a tear. '– here, inside my head.'

'That's awful,' said Tom.

'Oh, it's even worse than that, sir. He's brought his friends Mr Punjabootee, and Mr Robovich, and Mr Ching with him. They've turned this place into their own private social club.'

Tears began rolling down the manservant's

cheeks. Tom offered him a handkerchief to wipe his eyes. The man blew his nose into it loudly, before continuing.

'This used to be *my* mind, sir, and mine alone – the one place I could escape to where Mr Kruud couldn't call me a loser, where I could surround myself with happy memories and imagine a better life. I became very good at using my imagination like that, sir. But now I have to use it solely for the benefit of Mr Kruud and his friends. For a start, I've had to imagine huge private suites for all of them, and fill each one with their favourite things. So everything in Mr Kruud's suite is made from crisp white meringue. Of course, he never stops eating it. He's already gobbled down half a sofa and two bedside cabinets, so I'm constantly refurnishing it for him.' He shook his head, sadly. 'But that's not the worst of it. You see, the four of them spend most of their time in the games room on the top floor. Every day I have to imagine a new game, sometimes several, to keep them amused. But they're not satisfied with ordinary games. Oh no! They have to be special – befitting their position as billionaires. Yesterday they wanted to go bowling. But instead of using bowling balls and skittles, they thought it would be fun to send dragon's eggs crashing into priceless, thousand-year-old Ming vases. So I imagined it for them and five minutes later – after they'd smashed everything to bits and covered themselves in sticky green egg yolk – they complained of being bored and told me to imagine something else. And I can't refuse, or else they'll . . .'

The butler's head drooped, like a tired flower wilting on the end of its stalk.

'What's your name?' asked Polly.

'Digby,' the butler replied, raising his head wearily. 'Although Mr Kruud calls me Digby the Doormat, because he enjoys wiping his feet on me.'

The muffled sound of a gunshot, followed by distant laughter, wafted down from the top of the building, causing the diamond chandelier in the centre of the room to shake.

Digby looked up, nervously, before brushing a few specks of ceiling dust from his shoulder.

'Is the Grand Fizzler here, too?' asked Tom.

The butler pressed a finger to his lips.

'Shhh, I'm not allowed to talk about him, sir. His identity is a secret.'

'But is he here?' Tom whispered.

The butler nodded slowly, his mouth turning down steeply at the edges. Whoever the Grand Fizzler was, the butler clearly loathed him.

'Where?' demanded Polly.

Again the butler cast his eyes towards the ceiling.

'With them?'

He shook his head.

'Higher? In the attic?'

This time the butler nodded.

'Please don't say I told you, miss,' he pleaded quietly. 'I'm forbidden to say anything about him. If I do they've threatened to take all the memories I have of my mother and scatter them to the wind outside. Imagine not being able to remember your mother. Oh, deary me . . .'

Suddenly, a lump formed in Tom's throat. He understood perfectly. His own most precious memory was of his mother the day before she died – dancing around the living room with him in one hand and the vacuum cleaner in the other. Even the thought of losing it made him feel sick.

'Don't worry, Digby,' he told him. 'We won't tell anyone. But we must find the Grand Fizzler.'

'I wouldn't advise it, sir. Mr Kruud and his friends are on a hunting expedition in the games room. You'd have to find a way past them to reach the attic.'

'What are they hunting?' asked Polly.

'Something which even with their vast wealth they couldn't hunt in the real world, miss. Extinct species.'

'Like dinosaurs?' Polly asked.

'Oh deary me, no. Dinosaurs are far too common – everyone knows about them. They demanded to hunt extinct animals that ordinary folk haven't heard of. Luckily, I read a book about them once, so I've been able to imagine a whole forest full of them. Unfortunately, there were no pictures, so I've had to guess what everything looked like, but hopefully Mr Kruud and his friends won't know the difference. After all, who's to say that great elephant birds didn't have trunks? There's no one alive who's ever seen one.'

'Can you take us to the Grand Fizzler?'

'I daren't, sir. You know what they'll do to me if they find out. Mind you . . .' he added, rubbing his chin, 'I can imagine that the *animals* might want to help you. I could do that, I suppose . . .'

He took them as far as the lift.

'I'm afraid the lift goes only as far as the games room. You'll have to find your own way to the attic from there.'

They stepped inside, where the next Digby was ready to greet them, this time dressed in a lift boy's uniform. He caught Tom staring at him.

'You're right, sir. I'm smaller than Digby the Receptionist, and the receptionist is smaller than Digby the Doorman, and the doorman is smaller than . . . well, you get the idea. Just one of Mr Robovich's little jokes. He likes us to fit inside each other at night like a set of Russian dolls. He says it reminds him of home and that, besides, we take up less room that way. Less room!' he sobbed, clenching his frail, bony fists. 'This is *my* mind. It's supposed to belong to *me*!'

He pressed the top button, and the floor jerked upwards.

'Going up,' he sniffed.

The Flying Fortune Teller

The doors slid open. Polly and Tom peered out of the lift to find themselves stranded halfway up a canary-yellow tree trunk, almost twenty feet above the forest floor.

'I'm sorry,' whispered Digby. 'I couldn't help but imagine that both of you enjoy jumping out of trees – so here we are.'

Polly looked down, nervously.

'But please don't worry, miss,' Digby continued. 'I imagined that you like soft landings, too.'

Even so, it was a long drop. Polly gripped Tom's hand.

'Do you think it's possible to break a leg jumping out of an imaginary tree?' she asked him.

'Anything's possible,' he reminded her, 'but I suppose there's only one way to find out. Are you ready?'

Polly nodded, so they thanked Digby for his help and, on the count of three, they jumped.

Kruud's manservant was right. They landed safely on a soft, springy mattress of glowing orange and red leaves each shaped like a large lick of flame. They turned back to the trunk, on which was fixed a small brass plate bearing the name of the tree, followed by the year in which the last of its kind had been chopped down. 'Canary Dragon Tree, 1990', it read. Looking up, they saw no sign of the lift. In its place, above another brass plate which read 'Laughing Owl, 1914', there was a hole from which peered the face of a dishevelled, rather serious-looking owl. For a few moments the bird blinked at Polly and Tom, no doubt chewing over some morsel of owlish wisdom. Then, suddenly, it fell backwards, hooting with laughter as though someone had begun tickling it with one of its own feathers.

The owl's merriment wasn't the only sound to be heard. Digby had filled the trees with an orchestra of birds, so that the air vibrated with the sound of black-browed babblers babbling, Mangarevan whistlers whistling, and Alfaro's hummingbirds humming. Above, in the gaps between the trees, the sky was awash with colour, as flocks of long-extinct Cuban red macaws, yellow-billed pintails and pink-headed ducks arced across the bright-blue sky like huge, feathery rainbows. And on the ground, there was more colour, and more noise, as some of the strangest looking creatures that Polly and Tom had ever seen – such as desert rat-kangaroos, and Vietnam warty pigs, and great elephant birds – skipped and scampered, padded and prowled through the forest. Indeed, the warm air tingled not just with the presence of the Fizzle – which hung like a fine forest mist all around them – but with the excitement of the animals brought back to life – if only in Digby's imagination.

'This doesn't make any sense,' said Tom. 'Forests don't have attics. What are we supposed to do now?'

'According to Digby this is also the top floor,' Polly reminded him. 'So, whatever's above it must be the attic, mustn't it?'

Tom shrugged, so she continued.

'Maybe if we travel upwards until we can't go any higher, we'll find it.'

Tom couldn't think of a better plan, so he crouched low to the ground to study it for any sign of a slope, like a golfer lining up a putt. If only he knew what they were looking for . . .

Suddenly, he dropped on to his knees, his nose almost touching the forest floor as he studied one of the leaves on a nearby plant. Resting on it was a small brown moth, the pattern on its wings resembling a pair of dark, mysterious eyes. Like everything in the forest, the name by which it was known in Digby's book was clearly displayed, this time on a little white plastic stake stuck into the ground next to it. 'British Gypsy Moth, 1907' it read. A single drop of Fizzle lay like dew in the centre of the leaf, into which the moth appeared to be staring much as a gypsy might gaze into a crystal ball.

'Wow – do you think it's a fortune-teller?' whispered Polly, joining Tom on the ground and pressing her nose close to it.

'Anything's possible,' Tom conceded, although he didn't really believe that anyone, least of all a moth, could predict the future. But he did believe in the Fizzle, and perhaps it was trying to give them a clue. Surely the moth wouldn't have ventured out in the daylight for no reason? They wiggled closer to peer into the droplet. At first they could see nothing but their own reflections. But then something else appeared in the Fizzle's surface – a tiny mouse. For a moment it stopped preening its silver-grey fur and looked up at them. Then, suddenly, it was gone, as the crack of a gunshot shook the air, sending the gypsy moth into flight and her crystal ball rolling silently off the edge of the leaf. As it dripped on to the forest floor, Polly and Tom pressed themselves flat against the ground and listened. Amid the cacophony of fleeing animals a familiar voice – one which they had hoped never to hear again – rang out through the forest.

'Hey boys, I just shot me a red gazelle. Yes sireee! Accordin' to the tag on its collar, ain't no one seen one o' these since 1994. Yes siree!'

Before Tom could stop her, Polly had jumped to her feet.

'Get down!' he hissed, tugging her ankle. But it was too late.

'That's a wicked and horrible thing to do,' she called out. Kruud and his three associates looked up from their kill.

'What in the dollar-kissin' world are you –'

Tom jumped to his feet and grabbed Polly's arm.

'Come on, up's this way. We have to run.'

Polly came to her senses and stared, saucer-eyed, at the four hunters who had begun to walk towards them, shouting. She turned and ran. Swiping the undergrowth aside with her Fizzlestick, she and Tom hurtled through the trees until they found an overgrown forest path. As the shouting dimmed Polly paused to catch her breath.

'He's eaten . . . too many meringues,' she gasped.

Suddenly, the sound of rattling filled the air, as though a giant invisible rattlesnake was shaking its tail ready to strike. Behind them, as the cacophony threatened to shake the leaves off the surrounding trees, Kruud and his fellow hunters dropped their rifles and clutched their heads, their whole bodies contorted with pain as though it were they who were being shaken. Then, as the phantom rattler fell silent, Kruud retrieved his weapon and shook it angrily at the sky.

'We're goin' as fast as we damn well can,' he shouted, as though protesting at some unfair punishment. Then he beckoned his fellow hunters to continue the chase. But Polly and Tom had sped away again, and reached a junction in the forest path.

'Left . . . or right?' panted Polly.

Once again Tom crouched low to the ground.

'Up's that way,' he said, pointing. So they veered left. Sure enough, the path began to slope upwards, rising gently around the side of a hill. Halfway up they paused for breath again, ducking down behind some rocks. Tom peered out, checking the junction below for any sign of Kruud and his friends.

'They haven't reached it yet,' he whispered. 'Maybe they'll go the other way.'

But Polly didn't reply. He turned to find her standing in the mouth of a cave, which was set into the hillside just behind him. Her head was pushed forward into the gloom, and she was about to follow it. He leaped up and pulled her back, just as an enormous roar echoed around the inside.

'Polly!'

'I thought there might be another lift inside,' she explained.

'Look,' he said, pointing to a little brass plate attached to the side of the entrance. 'That was a cave bear, and there are also some –'

Before he could explain that the cave was also home to half a million ghost-faced bats, they flew out, spiralling upwards in a thick, furry-black cloud. Moments later, having agreed that thanks to Polly their alarm clock had gone off early, they returned. But as they whooshed back into the cave Tom noticed that one of them had fallen behind, having diverted briefly to pick up the enormous load which it carried below in its claws. Struggling to stay airborne it rose and fell in the air, but seemed determined to deliver its package. Finally, as it flew over Polly the bat dropped its cargo at her feet. She picked it up.

'It's a leaf,' she said, wrapping it around her waist as though she were sizing it up for a new costume, 'as big as a bath mat.'

'Perhaps it's another clue,' suggested Tom. 'Maybe we're supposed to find the tree that it came from and climb it.'

'It must be huge,' said Polly, more in anticipation than alarm. She rolled the leaf up into a tight tube and handed it to Tom, just as a paradise parrot swooped over their heads.

'K-k-k-kruuuuuud! K-k-k-kruuuuud!' it warned as it flew up the path ahead of them.

Instantly, Polly and Tom ducked behind the rocks then, slowly, peered out to watch as their pursuers reached the junction. Tom knew that if Kruud had guessed who they were looking for, he would already suspect that he and Polly had turned up the hill. And he was right. Pausing only to stuff a meringue into his mouth, Kruud turned left and followed them. Polly and Tom darted from the rocks and ran. As Kruud and his friends spotted them they merely quickened their pace, striding with a steady confidence as though they knew already where Polly and Tom were heading, and that their capture was inevitable.

As Polly and Tom reached the summit the path ended and the ground levelled out, as if the top of the hill had been sliced off with a giant carving knife. Sprouting from such even ground the trees grew tall and straight, evenly spaced and, at first glance, as uniform as the ground from which they grew. With no idea which way, if any, was up, Polly and Tom left the path behind and continued running towards the centre of the wood. As

Kruud's huge white cowboy hat appeared over the brow of the hill the parrot swooped overhead a second time.

'K-k-k-keep left! K-k-k-keep left!' it squawked.

Tom grabbed Polly's hand and pulled her after him, glancing down occasionally to note that the fallen leaves were still smaller than the one he was carrying. But as they sprinted past tree after tree the leaves appeared to be getting bigger. They had also begun to rustle. Suddenly the ground shuddered and something began to push out of the earth, spearing the leaves with its finger-long thorns as it grew. As the ancient thorn-bush rose either side of them it steered Polly and Tom this way and that, blocking them in with its impenetrable spikes as it led them along the path that it was creating. They could do nothing but follow it. Finally, it led them to a tree. As they reached it the bush sprang up like barbed wire each side of the trunk, trapping them in a dead end. Tom lifted a leaf from a nearby thorn on which it had been impaled, as if presented for his inspection. Then he unfurled the leaf dropped by the bat. The two were a perfect match. Polly turned to read the small brass plate attached to the trunk. 'Big-leafed Mahogany Tree', it read, '2005'.

'This could be it, Tom. The tallest tree on the highest hill. Maybe the attic's at the top.'

Still Tom wasn't convinced.

'But an attic is a room inside a house, isn't it? This is just a tree.'

As if to settle the debate, the parrot called out again from a nearby branch.

'C-c-c-climb, c-c-c-climb!'

But the advice came too late. The thorn bush had covered the entire hilltop, leaving nothing but a narrow trail along which, even now, Polly and Tom could see the hunters approaching. They backed up against the trunk. Then, suddenly, Kruud and his three fellow hunters spotted them. The thorn bushes did nothing to divert them, or block their path. Neither did those around Polly and Tom part to offer them an escape route. Even the tree to which they had been led looked impossible to climb, its wide, featureless trunk as smooth as a fireman's pole and so high that its dark-green canopy was shrouded in a cloudy, Fizzle-like mist hundreds of feet above them. They were trapped, and Kruud knew it. He and his friends slackened their pace, ambling along the track which the thorn bush had left open for them, as though they were enjoying a leisurely Sunday afternoon stroll.

Finally, Kruud swaggered to a halt a few metres in front of them, his hunting rifle slung menacingly over his shoulder. He plucked a thorn from the bush next to him and used it to dislodge a sticky piece of meringue from his front teeth, before flicking it back into the undergrowth.

'Howdy folks,' he said.

Sour Milk and Jelly Babies

'Well, lookee here – a pair of extinct trespassers,' Kruud sneered.

'We're not trespassers,' Polly corrected him, 'and we're not extinct.'

Kruud flipped another meringue into his mouth and glanced at his gun.

'Wanna bet?'

'We have to speak to the Grand Fizzler,' Polly demanded.

'He ain't here,' Kruud barked, his eyes flicking up at the tree for a split second – just long enough for Polly to notice. So she was right. The Grand Fizzler *was* up there.

'All we want to do is save Scarlett,' said Tom. 'Do you know where she is?'

Kruud tipped his head back and laughed. Then he glared at them, his face like a huge red-ripe tomato ready to burst.

'Hell, boy! As if I'd tell you. She and the rest of you dough-brained do-gooders blew up my Fizzle filter, destroyed my island an' ruined my business. Do you think I give a monkey's meringues what happens to any of you?'

'At least you're alive,' Polly insisted. 'Scarlett won't be unless we find her soon.'

Kruud's face grew even redder.

'You call this bein' alive?' he spat, spraying the air with meringue crumbs. ''Cause I sure as hell don't.'

'What do you mean?' Polly asked.

Kruud looked nervously up at the sky, and said nothing.

'What are you going to do to us?' said Tom.

Kruud smiled bitterly.

'Gee, I dunno. Let me see . . . Maybe I'll get Digby to imagine you both turning into crispy white meringue so I can bite off your fingers one by one. Or perhaps he can turn you into a huge bucket o' golf balls so I can spend the day hittin' you off the roof. I'm sure my friends will have a few suggestions, too. Perhaps they'd like to see you covered from head to toe in spiders, or stuck in a lift with a man-eatin' tiger, or tied together like a pair of elastic bands so that you have to spend eternity trying to unravel yourselves. Or all three at the same time. I'm sure I could arrange it. What d'ya think, boys?'

His associates nodded. It all sounded good.

'Or maybe,' he drawled, swinging the gun down from his shoulder, 'I'll just take ma revenge the good ol'-fashioned way.'

As he spoke, the thorn bush behind him began to move. Tom thought he heard the rumble of distant thunder, but a quick look at the sky poking through gaps in the trees showed it to be blue and clear. Kruud looked over his shoulder. At its far end the path appeared to be widening, as something impervious to the needlelike thorns pushed the bush aside, ploughing a wide furrow as it hurtled straight for them. Whatever it was, there was no way to avoid it.

Tom crouched down.

'Quick, Polly, climb on to my shoulders. See if there's anything up there that you can grab hold of.'

For a moment Polly and Tom forgot Kruud and the others, their only thoughts being to escape whatever was about to come crashing out of the bushes.

'Maybe there's something higher up that you can hook your Fizzlestick on to.'

But there was nothing. Frantically Polly swept the stick over the bark above her head, hoping it would catch some nook or cranny that would allow her to lift herself up. But there was not so much as a ripple in the surface. She turned to look back down the path.

'Tom, I can see something coming . . . oh no!'

At that moment Kruud, Punjabootee, Robovich and Ching came running towards them, hurling themselves into the thorn bushes either side as the massive beast thundered out of the undergrowth like an armoured truck. As the ground shook, Tom clasped Polly's ankles to keep her steady, knowing that if he let go, or began counting backwards to return to his cabin, she would fall into the path of whatever was about to flatten him. He closed his eyes, just as Polly's ear-splitting scream sent every bird squawking from the treetops. When he opened them a second later – surprised, indeed, that he still could – he found a small, silver-coloured mouse standing in front of his nose, sniffing the air and preening its whiskers. Even through crossed eyes Tom recognised it as the mouse that he and Polly had observed in the gypsy moth's crystal ball. It was perched on the tip of a long curved horn which belonged – according to the tag dangling from the beast's ear – to a woolly rhino. Thanks to Digby's imagination, the wool in question had been knitted into a rather fetching chain-mail sweater, currently covered in broken inch-long thorns. Suddenly the mouse leaped on to Tom's shoulder and the rhino backed away, snorting hot, angry air towards the four hunters whose painful groans had begun drifting up from deep inside the thorn bushes. Then, with a contemptuous flick of its ten-thousand-year-old tail, it stomped back into the undergrowth.

Polly and Tom's troubles were by no means over. One by one, the heads of the four hunters began to rise like prickly pears from the bushes. In a few minutes they would disentangle themselves.

'Jump down, Polly. We have to go.'

But Tom realised that he could no longer feel Polly's weight on his shoulders. He looked up to find her far above him, climbing the tree trunk. A long-extinct tree fungus had begun sprouting out of the bark, each grey-brown growth protruding from the trunk like a small shelf, allowing her to climb up. Tom turned to follow, hoping that the steps, which reminded him of giant mushrooms cut in half, would support his weight. But now he had no choice. Kruud emerged suddenly from the undergrowth like a giant white cactus, swollen with rage. Tom hauled himself up the first few steps just as Kruud reached up to grab his ankle.

'Wait a dollar-kissin' minute, boy. You ain't goin' nowhere.'

But Tom was too quick. Once again, the air

shook as the phantom rattler showed its displeasure, and Kruud and his associates fell to their knees clutching their heads.

'Dammit, we're doin' our best,' Kruud bellowed, before leaping back to his feet and making a clumsy lunge to follow Tom. As he stepped on to the first fungus shelf it crumbled under his foot and he fell back into the thorn bush. Roaring with pain, he lifted himself out, then rejoined his friends as they stretched their arms back into the undergrowth, inch by slow, thorny inch, to retrieve the guns which still lay there. But by the time they had rearmed themselves, Polly and Tom had disappeared into the mist and the thorn bush, its job done, retreated slowly into the soft earth from which it had sprung.

High above, Polly and Tom were joined by an imperial woodpecker which began tapping away at the wood to carve additional handholds for their climb. Stopping only to straighten the imperial crown which Digby's imagination had bestowed upon it, the ermine-winged woodpecker helped speed their progress so that within a few minutes they had reached the tree's dark-green canopy. As the foliage came within arm's reach a long furry tail lowered itself out of the leaves, its end curling upwards to form a hook. Polly hooked her Fizzlestick over it and allowed herself to be pulled up into the branches. Then it was Tom's turn, as the tails of two black spider monkeys reached down in front of him.

Polly had spent her life climbing trees on the Shipley Manor estate, but never had she seen one like this. Beneath the outer covering of giant leaves, the branches radiated out from the trunk in a series of flat, horizontal layers, each of which resembled a huge wooden spider's web. Each layer was within grasp of the slightly narrower one above, so that Polly and Tom were able to climb up as if through the framework of a building. With an occasional lift-up from the tree's chattering residents they quickly reached the final layer of branches. This was no more than a few metres wide and, from it, six wooden posts – one at each point around its hexagonal perimeter – rose like stilts through the leafy canopy above. Tom shuffled over to one of them and climbed it until his head disappeared through the leaves. He returned a few seconds later.

'There's a tree house up there,' he reported.

Polly's eyes brightened. For a moment she imagined the sort of house in which the Grand Fizzler might live – perhaps with crystal domes shaped like Fizzle droplets, and marbled halls, and multicoloured mosaic floors, and Fizzle fountains everywhere.

'It's just an ordinary tree house with a veranda running round it,' Tom said. 'Like something Slugbucket might build on the estate, only not as good.'

'It's not a palace?' said Polly.

Tom shook his head.

'No. In fact, the whole thing's not much bigger than a garden shed.'

For a moment Polly was disappointed, until she remembered why they were there. Quickly she followed Tom as he climbed up through the canopy. They clambered on to the veranda, bare except for a hard wooden chair overlooking the forest. From this viewpoint Tom could see that, with nothing but sky and cloud above them, they had indeed reached the highest point in the forest.

'This must be the attic, then,' said Polly. 'Let's go in.'

Tom knocked politely on the door, but Polly squeezed past him impatiently.

'Really, Tom! This is a matter of life and death.' She pushed the door open. There was no one inside.

'Fizzlesticks! He's not here. We've been tricked.'

She turned to leave, but Tom stepped through the doorway determined to take a closer look, so she followed him.

The hexagonal room was bare except for rows of

wooden shelves which lined four of the walls, each sagging like a ship's hammock under the weight of the containers which were crammed on to it. Slowly, Polly and Tom walked around the room. Each set of shelves appeared to hold a different kind of container. One wall was lined with milk bottles, the contents of which had long ago turned sour, or thickened into foul-smelling cheese, or shrunk into lumps of fur-covered mould like shrivelled-up mice. Tom removed the gold top from one of the bottles and sniffed, regretting it instantly. He put it back and moved to the next set of shelves, which were filled with thin glass tubes in which stood thousands of Chinese acupuncture needles, each tip coated with a coloured liquid, like a poison dart. The wall next to it was covered with glass kitchen jars, each full to the brim with brightly coloured powders which Tom guessed, quite rightly, to be Indian cooking spices. The last wall looked as though it belonged in a toy shop, the shelves heaving under the weight of hundreds of Russian dolls, each depicting a different character, such as a sailor, or a hunter, or a magician. Polly took this last one from its shelf and pulled it apart, finding in its centre a mini-magician no bigger than her little finger. She squeezed it, then touched it with her tongue. Yuk.

'It's a jelly baby,' she said, screwing up her nose.

'I've never liked the purple ones.'

Suddenly, Tom was reminded of the room in Hopper Hawkins's mind in which he kept his collection of sweet jars. The containers on these shelves were labelled in much the same way, each describing the ability that would be acquired if its contents were consumed. Many of these skills Polly and Tom would have liked to acquire themselves – the ability to speak several foreign languages, for example. But others, which the Grand Fizzler used expertly during his public performances, were more sinister: 'Ranting and Raving', 'Falsehood and Fakery', 'Lying', 'Cheating', 'Jiggery-pokery'. If any proof were needed that the Grand Fizzler was a fake it was right in front of them. Unfortunately, the Grand Fizzler wasn't – so their mission to save Scarlett appeared to be no further forward.

As they turned to leave, the little mouse leaped off Tom's shoulder on to one of the shelves and began winding its way from shelf to shelf towards the ceiling. At the top it perched on a container labelled 'Piloting a Submarine'. Tom watched it closely. The mouse was important, they knew that – the woolly rhinoceros had delivered it especially. So, perhaps it was trying to tell them something. Suddenly it reared up on its tiny hind legs and began to sniff the air above it. Tom looked closer and saw a small brass loop, about the size of a wedding ring, protruding from the ceiling. He rushed outside, returning a few seconds later with the chair.

'I think there's a door in the ceiling, Polly,' he said, pointing to the latch. 'See if you can reach it with your Fizzlestick.'

Polly jumped on to the chair and immediately hooked the end of her Fizzlestick through the loop. Then, before Tom could warn her, she pulled. As the heavy wooden trapdoor swung down like an executioner's axe he grabbed her, dragging her off the chair as it sliced through the air towards her head. They tumbled to the floor beneath a shower of dust.

'Thanks, Tom,' she gasped.

They looked up to find the door hanging limp from the ceiling, swaying gently like a pub sign in the breeze. Polly brushed herself off, then reached up with her Fizzlestick to pull down the light metal ladder that was attached to the door's underside. The steps telescoped silently to the floor and Tom, slowly and quietly, began to climb up with Polly hurrying him along from behind. At the top he waited for her to squeeze alongside him.

Then, together, they peered into the attic.

The Grand Fizzler

As they poked their heads through the hole in the attic floor they found themselves staring at a pair of sandalled feet. Their owner appeared not to notice his two visitors. Instead, with his golden Fizzlestick clutched in one hand, the Grand Fizzler was busily studying a sheet of paper clasped in the other, moving his lips silently as if trying to remember the words typed on it. Almost immediately Polly and Tom saw that they were not looking directly at the Grand Fizzler, but at a reflection in the full-length mirror which stood in front of the trapdoor. The Grand Fizzler had to be, they realised, standing behind them. They didn't turn. Instead, they continued to watch as, with an occasional glance at his notes, His Effervescence began to practise his speech. At first he spoke in a low, monotonous drone which Polly and Tom could barely hear. But gradually, as the speech progressed, his voice became louder until, halfway through it, his arms sprang suddenly to life and he began waving the paper in the air and banging the end of his Fizzlestick against the floorboards, to emphasise the urgency and importance of his words. Then, as he brought his pronouncement to its dramatic climax, the whole room vibrated and his words reached a deafening crescendo . . .

'. . . and the Dry-Mouths shall feel the full, howling fury of the Fizzle as it rises again from its slumber. But this time be warned – it will bring death and destruction to us all. For whilst the Dry-Mouths walk freely among us, none of us will be safe. Hailstones the size of cannon balls will rain down to crush and shatter their bones. But they shall also shatter ours. Shafts of Fizzle ice will fall from the sky like crystal javelins to skewer them. But they shall also skewer us. Huge Fizzle waterspouts will stalk the earth, sucking up everyone we love – our mothers and fathers, brothers and sisters, sons and daughters. They will devour our farms, our factories, our cities, they will suck up the land itself and all the goodness in it until the world is a dry, barren wasteland full of nothing but misery and despair. And all because Dry-Mouths remain in our midst. For they alone displease the Fizzle . . .'

The Grand Fizzler paused to catch his breath.

'. . . But the Fizzle has spoken to me,' he continued, 'and its message is clear. We must save ourselves before it is too late. Even as I speak it is replenishing itself, growing so that soon it may rise again, this time to punish all those who have defied its authority, and who remain outside our great Fizzle family, threatening us all. That is why, today, I appear before you to make an historic declaration. Because the time for action . . . *has arrived*!'

He slammed the Fizzlestick so hard against the floorboards that the mirror shook.

Polly gasped, and the reflection looked down at her. Slowly, Polly and Tom turned to face the real Grand Fizzler. But the figure standing behind them was not clothed in blue robes, but in a butler's uniform. Neither was his grey hair long, but short, crowned on top with a bald patch the size of a drinks mat. Now that they could see the two men side by side the true identity of the Grand Fizzler – even beneath his lavish disguise – became obvious.

'Digby!'

The butler nodded sadly.

'The mirror is a lie, sir. This is the real me . . . Digby. I don't want to dress up and call myself the

Grand Fizzler. But they make me. It was also Mr Kruud's idea to copy your Fizzlestick, miss. Playing the part, he calls it. He and his friends have even forced me to digest some of their own skills so that I sound convincing. That's why I can speak so many languages. Each time I need to learn something new I just have to sample the contents of one of those jars in the room below. Not that it's ever very pleasant. To learn to speak Chinese I had to stick acupuncture needles in my tongue until it looked like a pink pincushion. As for having to drink ten-year-old milk –' His mouth turned down at the corners even more than usual. 'Anyway, that's why the Grand Fizzler is so convincing. Sometimes even I forget that I'm only acting.'

'But why are you doing it?' asked Polly. 'Everything the Grand Fizzler says is a lie – the Fizzle would never hurt anyone.'

'I know that, miss, and so do Mr Kruud and his associates. But to them business is business, and the Fizzle is the greatest opportunity in history to make money. Since they joined forces shortly after Fizzle Friday I've been helping the company make a fortune. Demand and supply, you see – the Grand Fizzler creates the demand for all those toys and trinkets, and KPRC Industries supplies them. But that's only the beginning – they have far bigger plans . . .'

Digby knelt down and buried his face in his hands, whilst his blue-clad reflection remained standing, quietly studying his notes. Polly and Tom lifted themselves through the hatch and sat either side of the butler, their legs dangling into the room below.

'But it's wrong to tell all those lies,' said Tom, quietly. 'You have to refuse.'

The butler looked up.

'I daren't, sir. You know what they would do if I disobeyed them. My memories are all I have. If they destroy those I'll have nothing.' Another tear began to trickle down his cheek. 'I might as well be dead.'

'Can't you just kick them out?' asked Polly. 'Your mind belongs to you, doesn't it?'

'Does it, miss? When they not only tell me what to say and do, but what to imagine as well? Besides, there are four of them, and only one of me.'

Tom looked puzzled.

'But there's Digby the Doorman, and Digby the Receptionist, and Digby the Liftboy –'

'I know, sir, but we're all the same old me, Digby the Doormat, and I'm no match for Mr Kruud, let alone all four of them – just look at me!'

'But can't you just *imagine* kicking them out?' asked Polly. 'You're good at imagining things, aren't you?'

'Oh, I've tried, miss. And you're right. I can imagine everything from the beginning of time to the end of the universe. I can imagine worlds I've never visited, people I've never met, creatures I've never seen, adventures I've never had. But I can't – I just *can't* – imagine saying no to Mr Kruud.'

'Have you always been such a coward?' she asked him.

Tom frowned at her.

'Polly!'

She clamped a hand over her mouth, shocked by her own bluntness. She looked across at Digby, whose head had shrunk deep into his collar.

'Oops,' she said. 'Sorry.'

Slowly Digby emerged, his eyes cast down as though he wished the ground would open up and swallow him.

He nodded meekly. Ashamed. But then he looked up.

'Except when I was a boy,' he remembered. 'When I was about three years old I tried to ride my older brother's bicycle. I remember it had a squeaky wheel. Anyway, one morning I climbed on to it, then fell off straightaway and gashed my knee.' Digby shivered, remembering how it had stung. 'But I climbed back on and managed to pedal a few feet before falling off again and cutting my other knee. So I climbed back on again. By the end of the day I was covered from head to toe in cuts and bruises – but I could ride that bicycle. For weeks afterwards my mother called me Digby the Indestructible.' Suddenly, the butler smiled, albeit faintly.

'And then there was the time I forced a boy to return the dinner money that he'd stolen from my sister . . . and the day I rescued my uncle's cat from the roof . . . and the night I spent in a derelict house to see if it was haunted. Now I come to think of it, before I started working for Mr Kruud I was quite daring.'

'Digby the Daredevil!' cried Polly. 'And if you can remember all those other Digbys, they must be here somewhere in your mind, mustn't they? Perhaps if you can find them they'll help you fight Mr Kruud.'

'But they're just memories of who I used to be, miss. Locked away in my past. I'd be too scared even to look for them in case Mr Kruud found out and punished me. And if I did find them –' He shuddered. '– just imagine how disgusted they'd be with me. I don't deserve their help or anyone else's.' He bowed his head again. 'I'm a hopeless loser, just like Mr Kruud says.'

Polly thought for a moment.

'Then we'll kick them out for you,' she said.

Tom shook his head.

'Even if we could, they'd only come back as soon as we leave. Digby has to get rid of them himself.'

'But I can't, sir. How can I?'

As he spoke the little mouse appeared on Tom's shoulder and began sniffing the air nervously, as though a sudden storm was about to engulf them.

'I see you've made friends with the silver key mouse,' said Digby. 'According to my book they used to run around all over Australia when I was a boy.'

Suddenly the mouse leaped on to the floorboards and scurried towards him, before climbing up the outside of his trouser leg and into the snug safety of his jacket pocket. And not a moment too soon.

As it disappeared from view the sound of rattling filled the air outside. Moments later an even more ominous noise joined it, which reminded Polly of Slugbucket's snoring. Instantly, she knew what it was. Sawing. As the screaming chainsaw started to slice through the tree's ancient trunk a hundred feet below, vibrations spread upwards through the branches, growing with intensity until they reached the tree house at the top. There, with nowhere further to go, they made the walls tremble and dust dance on the floorboards.

Then, the rattling and the sawing stopped.

For a few seconds there was silence, as every

animal stopped what it was doing and pricked up its ears, ready to run.

Then Kruud's triumphant voice wafted up through the branches, confirming their worst fears.

'Timmm-berrrr!'

The tree started to creak, straining first this way then that as it decided which way to fall. Quickly, Polly and Tom climbed down the ladder into the room below. Tom called up to the butler, whose head appeared in the open hatch.

'Don't worry about me, sir – I'll just imagine moving to an identical tree house next door. I'll be quite safe.'

Suddenly the tree house tilted to one side, sending every acupuncture needle, milk bottle and glass jar flying off the shelves. The containers exploded on the floor, instantly filling the room with coloured clouds of eye-watering curry powder and the stench of putrefying milk. Their eyes burning, Polly and Tom stumbled through the doorway and emerged, choking, on to the veranda. Immediately Polly ran for the steps but Tom turned, plunging his head back into the curry cloud from which they had just escaped. There was one last thing he had to know.

'Digby! What is the Grand Fizzler's declaration? How does your speech end?'

Reluctantly, the butler's quiet, quivering voice

drifted down from the attic, so weighed down with shame that it barely reached him.

'Badly, sir,' he said. 'I'm going to declare –'

Suddenly, Tom was yanked backwards by his shirt as a shower of needles flew past him into the forest.

'Come on, Tom! We have to jump to the next tree, if we can –'

But before Polly could finish her sentence the floor of the veranda buckled and both of them were hurled against the bamboo railings. Secured with nothing more than strands of twisted vine, the railings gave way instantly, and Polly and Tom swung out into the forest, still clinging to what bamboo remained attached to the veranda. There they dangled, like washing hung out to dry, as the final few threads of vine holding them to the tree house began to unravel. Suddenly there was an enormous crack, and the thousand-year-old tree began slowly to fall, moaning and creaking, through its neighbours. As Polly and Tom fell with it, they could do nothing but hang on to the bamboo and each other. Finally, as spider monkeys screamed in terror around them – baring their teeth at an enemy they could not see, let alone fight – the ground came up to meet them. Tom closed his eyes.

'Count backwards, Polly, count ba –'

As he hit the soft mattress of leaves on the forest floor Tom imagined it to be his bunk. He imagined the gentle roll of the ocean beneath Shipley Manor and the smell of salty air wafting in through his porthole. When he opened his eyes a moment later, he was back in his cabin. Polly was at his side, rubbing her eyes. Their hearts pounding with excitement – despite not having moved an inch from the bunk throughout their adventure – they checked their arms and legs for the numerous cuts and bruises which had felt so real during their fall. But there wasn't a scratch on either of them. Polly leaped up.

'Come on, we have to tell the Captain.'

Blue Riders

Scarlett had been climbing, too. Her journey up the cliff face had taken her five days and nights, but now she was at the top, with only her cargo to haul the last few feet after her. She wedged her feet against the snow-covered rock and heaved on the rope until she was lying on her back. Then, passing the rope through her hands, she pulled herself upright, gripped it tight and leaned back again. With one final tug the bundle which she had pulled up the cliff face came into view and rolled over on to the top. She lay back in the snow. The climb had exhausted her. But she had thought that she had no other choice. Her great-grandfather Hopper Hawkins had taught her never to leave her plane if she crashed. But he had also taught her to think for herself. And that is what she had done. The wreckage of her plane lay concealed in the shadow of the cliff against which it had exploded. There was no way it would ever have been spotted. Even the distress flares in the survival kit wouldn't have reached the top of the cliff, so no search plane except one travelling directly overhead would be able to see it. And why would a search plane do that when she was so far off course?

No. She and her plane were unlikely to be found – at least not before she had frozen to death. She would have to climb out. But she had been wrong. Barely had she begun her climb when an Ice Patrol plane – alerted by a strange call from an English sea captain – had started to circle the area. She had hauled the bundle up to her as fast as she could, tearing off her gloves to dig out a distress flare from it. But she had been too late, firing the bright orange flare skyward just as the plane's tail disappeared over the rim of the cliff. Scarlett knew that the plane wouldn't return, so she had kept climbing. Now, as she lay among the rocks at the top, sheltered from the icy wind, she allowed herself the luxury of a few minutes to rest and reflect on the events of the past five days, and to take stock of her provisions.

The main part of the bundle that she had hauled up the cliff face was, in fact, the back seat of her plane. Having retrieved the ice saw and her jacket – which the bear had abandoned with her bag of toffees still in the pocket – she had found the aircraft lying in two pieces at the base of the cliff. The front half was a charred and mangled wreck, but the tail had snapped off on impact and been flung clear of the inferno. Inside it she had found the green survival kit, and retrieved food rations, some distress flares, a tin cup, matches and a magnifying glass. Hopper's old parachute – which she carried mostly for luck, knowing that Hopper had never had to use it – had survived and would, she knew, make an excellent tent. Apart from that there were two mooring ropes – which normally she used to anchor the plane in high winds – and the back seat. From this she had removed the thick padded base, slitting it open so that later she would be able to use it as a makeshift sleeping bag. Until then she would use it to carry the contents of the survival box.

Then she noticed that a section of the tail fin had smashed off. If she could haul it up the cliff face she knew that it would make an excellent sledge, or a groundsheet, or even a mirror to glint into the eye of a passing pilot. So she had tied the seat to it and, with the other end of the rope secured around her waist, had begun to climb. When she felt the rope tighten she had wedged herself into one of the many crevices in the cliff face and pulled the heavy load up after her. Then, having pushed the bundle into the crevice, she would continue, wriggling the bundle free and hauling it up after her each time the rope tightened. At night, if there was no moon to light her way, she would wedge herself deep into a crevice and pull the foam bundle in after her to seal her off from the wind. Then, the next day, she would start again.

The cliff face yielded little to aid her on the way, but she made use of what there was, resting whenever she encountered a narrow ledge, and gathering up the twiggy walls of abandoned tern's nests. These she would stuff into her jacket to provide extra insulation, or burn to make small fires that would last just long enough for her to thaw out the most vital pieces of her climbing equipment – her fingers and toes. If they froze, Scarlett knew, the rest of her would, too. On every such fire she would melt a cupful of snow to make drinking water, keeping the hot metal pressed between her hands afterwards to absorb as much of its warmth into her fingers as she could, before resuming the climb. Fortunately, whilst pockets of snow had gathered in the cliff's nooks and crannies – enough to provide her with sufficient drinking water – most of the cliff face was swept bare by the wind. When, at last, she had hauled herself to the top she was exhausted, and hungry enough to eat an entire polar bear, but at least she was dry.

Resting now among the rocks, she looked up as the sun made a brief appearance between the clouds. Feeling its warmth on her face, and with her supply of matches dwindling, she knew that this was an opportunity not to be missed. Quickly, Scarlett tipped a handful of snow into the tin cup and sat it on a flat rock, before taking out the magnifying glass and placing it over the top. Whilst she waited for the snow inside to melt under the magnified warmth of the sun she looked down at the lake below, its curved, crystal-clear surface glistening under the same sunlight. Then she looked back at the magnifying glass covering the tin cup. Then back at the ice covering the lake. Snap, she thought.

A few minutes later, having drained her cup, she left the shelter of the rocks. The land rose gently away from the cliff edge towards two tall peaks. In between, a short distance away, a band of trees circled the cliff edge like a dog collar. Pulling the tail fin behind her like a sledge she would drag her survival kit into the trees and set up shelter before nightfall. She would light a huge fire to keep herself warm and safe through the night. Then in the morning, rested and refreshed, she would set out on the long hike down to the coastline on the other side of the mountains. She knew the search for her would still be going on there and that she would have some chance of being spotted, or at least of finding some kind of settlement.

That night, cocooned in her shelter with her socks and gloves drying by the fire outside, Scarlett recalled how her grandfather had swum to her rescue five days before. Trapped under the ice with no idea how to find her way out, she had wished for him and, suddenly, he had appeared, exactly as she remembered him. Smiling, he had swum to her and taken her by the hand. Then he had led her to the hole in the ice. As she clambered out, warm and dry, she had turned, reaching back for his hand. Somehow it slipped through her grasp and he had disappeared like a ghost, back into the darkness. Then she had opened her fist to find his gold wedding ring resting there. Straightaway it had begun to dissolve, disintegrating into a million tiny creatures, each identical, each symmetrical, each able to join seamlessly with its neighbour to form the shape of their choosing. As Scarlett held the creatures in her palm the Fizzle gas had connected them to her. In that instant, as she let them trickle, tingling, through her fingers back into the water, her mind and theirs had become one, and she had understood – she had understood everything.

Early the next day Scarlett was awoken by the sound of motors. Rescue. She leaped up and ran towards the noise. As she neared the edge of the woods she caught a glimpse of four gold-coloured snowmobiles speeding towards the trees a few hundred metres away. Each was pulling a sledge piled high with what looked like wooden signposts. She raced to meet them, stumbling occasionally as she tried to run too fast through the deep snow. When they reached the wood the snowmobiles began snaking fast through the trees. Scarlett changed course to intercept them, screaming as loud as her cracked lips would allow. But their engines drowned out all other sound, the fur-lined hoods of their riders shielding from view all that was not directly in their path. They were approaching fast. If they passed her by, who knows where they would go – perhaps this was her one chance of survival. She would have to place herself in front of them. She stumbled on, watching the flashes of gold as they passed between the columns of trees in front of her.

As she ran closer the flashes became streaks as the number of trees between them decreased. And then she was there – a few more steps and their paths would cross. Suddenly, Scarlett threw herself face down into the snow and lay motionless. As they approached she had caught a glimpse of the lead rider. Beneath his fur coat she had seen the telltale shimmer of the blue robes worn by followers of the Grand Fizzler – and painted on the side of his snowmobile were the letters KPRC. Though she was cold and exhausted and weak with hunger, Scarlett's instinct was to hide. Everything that she had learned about the Grand Fizzler and his followers, and the connection between them and KPRC Industries, had left her in no doubt that they were the enemy. The snowmobiles passed, but just as she thought she was safe she heard them slow down and stop. There was nothing she could do except keep still – her face numb, yet burning with cold at the same time. Footsteps approached, a soft, barely audible crunch above the low, monotonous chug of the motors. Then a sudden, heart-stopping thud as one of the wooden signs was thrown back on to the sledge from which it had fallen. Finally, the engines roared into life again and the four sledges continued on their way leaving specks of oil – like spattered blood – behind them in the snow.

Scarlett waited until their engines sounded no louder than the drone of a distant bumble bee, before returning to her camp. She stuffed her pockets with whatever she could carry and packed the rest into the silky white camouflage of the shelter before setting off to follow them. She retraced her steps, stopping occasionally to ruffle the snow with a branch to conceal her tracks, and to carve discreet signals to herself on the tree trunks so that she, and she alone, would be able to find her camp. Then, as she reached the sledge marks she set off in pursuit, stepping carefully inside the tracks so that, should the snowmobiles return by the same route, she would have left no sign of her presence.

As she reached the perimeter of the trees the sledge tracks divided, with two sledges veering left and two right around the cliff edge. From behind a tree she watched as each sledge placed itself around the perimeter of the huge circular abyss like the four points of a compass. Then they began to move in short steps around it, stopping and starting as each driver unloaded another sign and hammered it into the ground. In an hour the circle was complete, and the sledges were empty of their cargo. Then, one by one, the engines revved and the Grand Fizzler's fur-clad followers retraced their steps. Scarlett pressed herself against the tree as they roared past her, and waited for silence to return. Then she made her way towards the cliff edge. The thin wooden signs gave a clear message that the new owner of the lake considered it to be out of bounds. 'Private Property – Keep Out,' they said, 'by order of KPRC Industries.'

Scarlett stared at them for a moment, then waded through the snow to the nearest sign. No one owns the Fizzle, she thought, wiggling it out of the ground. Then she trudged over to the next and heaved that out, too. The two posts would burn well on her campfire, she had decided, and she had an even better use for the rectangular signs on top.

'Emergency snow-shoes,' she muttered under her frosty breath, 'by order of Scarlett Hawkins.'

An hour later, having dried her clothes, she loaded her belongings and a stack of firewood on to the tail fin. Then, with her new snowshoes tied securely to the underside of her boots, she began dragging the makeshift sledge towards the tracks left by the snowmobiles. These she followed out of the comfort of the woods, climbing in slow, trudging steps towards the gap in the mountains. Finally, with the peaks rearing up each side of her like giant gatekeepers, she was able at last to glimpse the sea, a glittering triangle through the gap between them. She anchored the sledge and climbed the last few metres alone, eager to see the shoreline.

For a moment all thoughts of rescue, all feelings of cold and exhaustion and hunger were banished as she gazed down on the vast armada of icebergs drifting south from the coast. One of them in particular had attracted her attention. A hole had melted through its centre to create an archway which tapered to a point at the top, like the noses of two pirouetting ice dolphins nuzzled together in greeting. But it was what Scarlett could see through the archway which had stopped her in her tracks. Gleaming white against the dark-blue sea, its familiar shape was unmistakable. Kruud's yacht.

The Fizzle Factory

'Land ahoy!'

Slugbucket's voice rang out loud and clear from the Crow's Nest. Two days had passed since Polly and Tom had come crashing out of Digby's imagination. For most of the journey the Captain had held a steady course, but no longer. Progress was slow. The sea in front of Shipley Manor had become an obstacle course as acres of blinding white sea-ice and towering icebergs conspired to block their path. For the past day and a half, Polly, Tom and Moolah – with Grub, nodding and eager at her side – had between them kept constant watch from the roof. Leaning over the old stone walls, their breath freezing in the ice-cold Arctic air, they had guided the house, groaning and creaking, through the narrowest of passages, whilst Slugbucket scanned the horizon for distant hazards.

'Pack ice ten miles north,' he would call out from the Crow's Nest. 'Iceberg twenty miles east, driftin' west on collision course.'

And the Captain would respond, weaving Shipley Manor through the icy obstacle course as though he were tiptoeing down a muddy, puddle-strewn lane.

Land was still some way off but clearly visible now – a thin white line sandwiched between sky and sea, along which the mountain peaks rose and fell like the blip, blip, blips of a heartbeat. On the Captain's insistence the Ice Patrol had, several days earlier, flown over those same mountains and found no sign of Scarlett. But Polly and Tom were certain that she and the Fizzle were there. The Captain sailed the house as close to the shore as he could. Then, as the gaps between the ice sheets became impassable, he brought the great paddle wheels grinding to a halt, pulled the collar of his coat up around his ears and stepped out of the conservatory.

'Freezing Fizzlefish!' he shivered, joining his shipmates on the roof. 'I'm beginning to wish I hadn't shaved off my beard.'

Together, wrapped in several layers of warm clothing, they scanned the horizon for any sign of Scarlett. Suddenly, Polly spotted an old friend. A group of seals had gathered on a nearby ice sheet to eat the fish that they'd caught for their tea. But one of them stood apart. For, whilst it looked no different from the others, it had leaped on to the ice with its catch balanced perfectly on its nose. Polly watched as, like a seasoned circus performer, the seal flicked its head back and sent the fish somersaulting into the air, before swallowing it whole.

'That's Arthur, Mr Kruud's pet seal,' she said, pointing. 'Over there, look.'

Slugbucket had seen it too, and within a few seconds had found its owner's yacht, nestling amid the icebergs on the other side of a small peninsula.

'Polly's roight, Cap'n – 'is yacht's jus' over there.'

The Captain frowned.

'I suppose that explains why no one's been able to find the scoundrel – he's been hiding out on the high seas.'

'We need to ask him about Scarlett,' said Polly.

'P'raps he's already got 'er,' said Slugbucket. 'Prisoner, loik.'

'Either way I think it's time we found out. Is that old gypsy caravan of yours ready to set sail, Slugbucket?'

'It's shipshape an' rarin' ter go, Cap'n. Oi gave it a fresh coat o' waterproof paint only yesterday.'

With Moolah's help, Slugbucket began to winch the caravan off the roof and over the wall, ready to be lowered.

'I'm coming too,' Polly announced. But the Captain had other ideas.

'No, you're not, Polly. I want you and Tom to stay here and keep watch for Scarlett from the Crow's Nest.'

Then he jumped on to the wall and joined Slugbucket, Moolah and Mr Grub on the caravan steps. As Tom lowered it into the narrow water-channel three floors below, he called up.

'And keep trying to communicate with her. If you find out where Scarlett is, fly a flag from the Crow's Nest and we'll head straight back.'

Tom nodded grimly, knowing that already two days had passed since he and Polly had last heard a call for help.

As soon as the caravan hit the water, Slugbucket started the small outboard motor which he and Seymour had fitted to the back, and it began to zigzag through the ice towards Kruud's yacht.

Polly raced up to the Crow's Nest, snatching up the Captain's telescope from the desk to watch the caravan thread its way through the narrow water-channels. Then, as it reached the yacht, she saw four tiny figures emerge from it and climb the long gangplank into the side of the vessel.

Moments later, from around the other side of the yacht, she saw something else.

'Tom, there's a submarine – look!'

She handed him the telescope. Through it, he could see a sleek black submarine emerging from behind the yacht. A glass observation dome protruded like a hump from its back, large enough to accommodate several underwater sightseers.

'We have to stop it, Tom! Scarlett may be on board.'

'Perhaps we should fly the flag then – like the Captain told us to,' Tom suggested, returning the telescope to her eager hands.

'But they won't see it, Tom, they're all inside now. That's odd – the submarine's heading straight for the shore, as though it's going to crash into it. Now it's diving. We have to do something, Tom. It's getting away!'

Polly watched as the submarine sank slowly into the water, until all that remained above the surface was the observation dome. For a moment it appeared to float on the surface like a giant bubble, before following the rest of the submarine below the waves.

'That's it – a bubble.'

Suddenly, Polly had grabbed her Fizzlestick and, before Tom could stop her, had disappeared down the helter-skelter. He didn't catch up with her until she'd reached the roof, and by then it was too late. Already her feet were dangling over the ocean as she sat on top of Seymour's organic aerial bombardment launching device – the huge slide which hung over the outer wall. Several months previously they had launched an aerial barrage of flying fruit from it. Now, Polly was about to launch herself. Tom sprinted towards her, uncertain whether the contraption would still work.

'Don't do it, Polly!'

But she let go. Tom reached the wall just in time to watch her hurtle down the slide, looping the loop twice before setting off the trigger which raised the hoop at the bottom. As it sprang to attention ready to launch its passenger into the sky, Tom knew that if the Fizzle Flying Formula in the reservoir at the bottom had run out, Polly would fall to her death.

'Polly!'

Polly reached the foot of the slide in a blur, curving upwards as she passed through the hoop. For a moment Tom's eyes watered in the cold, so that he couldn't see the thin Fizzle skin stretched around her. But then it broke free and sealed itself, enclosing Polly in a perfectly formed bubble. She remembered Tom saying that flying a bubble was like riding a bike. He had meant that it was easy once you got the hang of it, but Polly had misunderstood and had begun pedalling her legs, her fists clenched around her Fizzlestick as though it were a pair of handlebars. The movement made her spin forward, tumbling over and over away from the house, out of control. He would have to go after her. He peered over the wall, hoping in vain to see the telltale glint of Fizzle Flying Formula catching the light at the bottom of the slide. Then he looked back out to sea to find Polly already halfway to the shore, unable to turn back. Nervously, he climbed the steps to the top of the slide. Then he pulled his thick coat tight around him, crossed his fingers . . . and let go.

Whoosh. A second later he was spinning into the sky inside his own Fizzle bubble. He relaxed every muscle in his body so that it stopped. Then he hung in the air for a few moments whilst his stomach settled, before stretching his arms out in front of him, and tensing his muscles again. Immediately the bubble responded and moved forward, so that within a few seconds he had caught up with Polly.

'Stop pedalling, Polly,' he called out to her as he floated past. 'Copy me and remember, if these bubbles touch anything, even each other, they'll burst. So we have to keep our distance.'

She nodded, her mouth crooked with concentration as she gained control. Tom led the way, glancing back every few seconds to check that Polly wasn't too close. Then he turned gently, hoping to guide her back to Shipley Manor and safety. But Polly refused to turn with him.

'I'm going to find Scarlett,' she yelled, continuing on. 'You can't stop me.'

And she was right. Tom had no choice but to double back and follow her. He turned, and together they headed for the last place where they had seen the submarine. Polly circled over the water, puzzled that she could see no trace of it in any direction. Then she continued on straight, flying across the shoreline and up the snowy slope towards a gap between two of the mountains. As they approached it Tom could hear the wind whistling around him, but he couldn't feel it. The inside of the bubble was warm and still, reminding him of car journeys on blustery days. As they passed through the gap the ring of trees came into view, then the huge hole which lay inside it. Polly and Tom circled around the rim looking for wreckage, then hovered above its centre while Tom demonstrated the crouching position which would allow them both to sink slowly into the abyss. Finally, they began to float down, gazing awestruck at the massive ice sheet covering the lake below, and the sheer cliff wall as it rose around them.

'Wow,' said Polly, 'someone must have pulled the plug out.'

Halfway down they spotted the charred remains

of Scarlett's plane. Together they flew down, and floated a few metres above the wreckage calling her name. Then Tom saw something move inside the plane's severed tail.

'Scarlett!'

He swooped down just as a head emerged from it. Then Polly screamed, and he launched himself back up again as the polar bear leaped into the open, reaching up on its hind legs to swipe at him with its long claws.

Suddenly Tom felt sick. No wonder he hadn't heard Scarlett's voice for the past few days. The polar bear must have –

Polly had come to the same conclusion. Together they hung limp in the air, drifting slowly upwards as the wreckage of Scarlett's plane gradually sank back into the shadows.

'Oh, poor Scarlett . . .'

As they reached the top of the cliff the grief became too much for Polly. Tears streaming down her face, she opened her mouth wide and sent a cry ripping through the air.

'Scarrrrletttt!'

'Yes?'

Polly and Tom looked down. A figure had stepped from behind a tree on the edge of the woods. Although she was wrapped in a piece of thick foam tied with rope around her waist, there was no mistaking Hopper Hawkins's old flying hat, or the explosion of rust-red curls bursting out from under it. Scarlett.

Polly reached out for her and the bubble shot towards the tree.

'Polly, watch out!' cried Tom. But he was too late. As Polly's bubble touched one of the overhanging branches it burst and she fell, landing with a muffled thud deep into a nearby snowdrift.

Instinctively, Tom landed beside her, his flying bubble turning into a flurry of miniature snowflakes as it popped.

A moment later Scarlett bounded across on her snowshoes to join him, and together they peered into the snowdrift.

'Are you all right, Polly?' asked Tom.

Slowly, Polly's arm reached up out of the snow and clasped his hand. Then, like a ghost emerging from a snowy grave, she pulled herself back on to her feet, and began brushing the snow from her clothes.

'I want to do that *again*,' she said, reaching back into the hole to retrieve her Fizzlestick. But Scarlett didn't smile. She had survived the past week by conserving every morsel of energy – and it was running out, fast.

'We thought the polar bear had eaten you,' said Tom.

'It nearly did,' Scarlett replied, 'but my great-grandfather saved me.'

She looked at Polly and Tom's puzzled faces.

'I'll explain later,' she said. 'First we need to collect as many of those signposts as we can for the fire. You'll both need snowshoes, too. Come on.'

Tom hesitated for a moment. Even though keeping warm might have been a matter of life and death, pulling other people's 'Private Property' signs out of the ground still felt, well, wrong.

'Come on, slowcoach,' said Polly. 'I bet you can't carry more than two.'

He shrugged, and despite feeling as though he shouldn't, proceeded to heave four posts out of the snow and sling two over each shoulder. They didn't speak again until they'd reached Scarlett's camp. Even then, Scarlett's priorities were clear – build up the fire and dry Polly's clothes. Only then, as Polly and Tom huddled under the shelter making their own snowshoes, did they tell her all about Digby.

'That doesn't surprise me,' she had responded finally. 'Kruud always uses other people to do his dirty work for him.'

Then, she had gone on to tell them her own story.

She hadn't given herself up to the riders, nor walked to the coast to hand herself over to Kruud, whom she assumed to be on board his yacht. Instead, she had decided to stay hidden for as long as possible to find out what mischief he was up to. Then she went on to explain how the tiny creatures in the lake – Pixelfish as she called them – had saved her and how, as they had dissolved slowly in her hand, she had had a brief glimpse into their own mind and understood why they were there.

'The lake is an enormous Fizzle factory,' she explained, 'and the Pixelfish are its workers – toiling away like bees inside a vast beehive. But their job isn't to make honey. It's to make people feel connected to each other. So, for the past million years the Pixelfish have been busy breathing in the seawater which flows into the lake and breathing out bubbles of the special gas which converts it into Fizzle.'

'So the Fizzle isn't magic, after all?' asked Polly.

'Of course it is!' Scarlett replied. 'Fantastic, stupendous, spellbinding magic. Only the master magician is . . . nature.'

She threw another signpost on the fire.

'But that's not all. The Pixelfish have become so good at connecting things that they can connect their bodies together, too. Even though each one is a tiny individual, capable of adjusting its colour like a dot on a television screen, they all share the same hexagonal shape which allows them to interlock like perfectly fitting building blocks. They can conjure up any shape you can imagine. And because their minds are connected to each other's as well as ours, whatever form they take acts and moves as one, to create the ultimate illusion. My great-grandfather's smile was exactly as I remembered it, right down to the wiggle of his moustache.'

'What I don't understand is why – apart from a few leaks now and then – the Fizzle rained down on Fizzle Friday and not some other time, like a hundred years from now,' said Polly.

'I'll show you,' said Scarlett, retrieving her tin cup from the shelter.

'Does your mother ever check whether Calypso's ill by putting a hand on her forehead?'

Polly nodded.

'Yes. And if she has a temperature mum will give her some medicine.'

'Well, the Fizzle knew when to fall using the same method – look.'

Scarlett snapped the tip of an icicle from a nearby branch and placed it in the bottom of the cup.

'Imagine the tin cup is the lake, full of Fizzle,' she explained, 'and at the bottom is a hole which is plugged up with ice to stop it draining away. Now watch.'

She took Hopper's old magnifying glass out of her jacket and placed it over the cup as though it were the ice covering the lake.

'Last year the earth warmed up so much that during the summer the snow which had covered the lake for thousands of years finally melted away. But the ice on top isn't flat, you see. Its surface is curved, like this magnifying glass.'

Polly and Tom watched closely as the icicle at the bottom of the cup slowly began to melt.

'You see, the sun's rays are being focused through the magnifying glass to meet in a single, burning point at the bottom of the cup. A block of ice embedded in the bottom of the lake like a huge frozen plug melted in exactly the same way. And as soon as it disappeared the water flooded through the hole, injecting itself into the earth's crust as the ice on top pushed it down, taking that poor stranded polar bear with it. After that there was no stopping it. The Fizzle spread out, filling up the network of underground reservoirs around the world – like the one beneath Dollar Island – before finally erupting on Fizzle Friday.'

'So the Fizzle is like a medicine?' asked Tom.

'That's right. To help us get on better, co-operate more, work together to make the earth healthy again. Because we haven't been looking after it properly. We've choked the skies with so much pollution that it's caught a fever hot enough to melt a glacier. The snow melting was the trigger, you see. It showed that the earth was sick and that it was time to administer the cure.'

Demonstration over, she returned the magnifying glass to her pocket.

'And it was working, too, until this bleary-eyed old beardycoot the Grand Fizzler or whatever he calls himself began poisoning everyone against each other. So now, instead of working side by side to make the earth well again, everyone's wasting their time worrying about who's Got the Fizzle and who's a Dry-Mouth. Talk about a fly in the ointment. He's up to something, too – I've been watching him.'

'You mean he's here?'

'Oh yes,' Scarlett replied, 'he's very big around these parts. In fact,' she continued, glancing up at the fading light, 'I think it's time I took you to see him.'

Half an hour later, Scarlett, Polly and Tom made their way back to the lake. As they reached the edge of the forest they heard the sound of snowmobiles.

'Quick, get down,' said Scarlett.

'Who are they?' whispered Polly.

'Bamboo-masters,' Scarlett replied. 'Only now they look like followers of the Grand Fizzler. They've been buzzing around the top of the cliff for the past two days. I think His Effervescence is about to make some sort of announcement. He's been rehearsing.'

'Where?' asked Polly.

'Down there,' said Scarlett, pointing towards the lake. 'Follow me.'

Crouching low, with Polly and Tom close behind, she shuffled across the expanse of snow between the trees and the cliff face. The three of them hid amongst a group of rocks close to the edge. Scarlett looked back at the mountains, silhouetted against the reddish glow of the setting sun.

'It shouldn't be long now,' she said, shuffling on her tummy to the edge of the cliff. Polly and Tom joined her, and the three of them peered down into the inky evening gloom.

'Do you remember that I said the ice on the lake was like a giant magnifying glass?'

They both nodded.

'Well, of course, focusing the sun's rays is only one thing a magnifying glass does.' She looked at her watch. 'I think it's about time.'

Suddenly below them the ice began to flash like a vast, flickering light bulb. After a few seconds it stopped, and staring up at them, his shining face spread a mile wide across the surface of the lake as though he were peering out from a huge circular cinema screen, was the Grand Fizzler.

'That tiny freckle on his nose,' Scarlett told them, 'isn't a freckle at all. It's the hole I dug in the ice a week ago.'

'His face is so huge,' gasped Polly.

'It's just an illusion,' Scarlett continued. 'The Grand Fizzler must be at the bottom of the lake and the frozen Fizzle on top is enlarging his face, just like a real magnifying glass. Somehow it can magnify his voice, too. It's quite a trick.'

'The submarine!' said Polly. 'I remember it had a funny glass bubble on top for looking at all the fish. He must be sitting in it all lit up, looking up at us.'

'But how did he get there?' wondered Tom, looking around at the sheer cliff walls.

'The same way the seawater gets into the lake,' replied Polly. 'There must be a secret tunnel or something which runs under the mountains and joins the lake to the sea.'

'Shhh,' Scarlett put a finger to her lips. 'He's about to start.'

The Grand Fizzler cleared his throat. Then he looked up – his huge smiling face shining like the moon.

'Welcome,' he droned, before shaking his head and mumbling to himself in Digby's thin, quivering voice.

'Deary me, that won't do at all. They wanted the

beginning to have more oomph, didn't they?'

He cleared his throat a second time, before taking a deep breath.

'Welcome to my home!' he boomed, this time sending hundreds of Arctic terns squawking from their nests on the cliff face. 'As you can see – I am the Fizzle, and the Fizzle is me. We are one. We are *all* one.'

He paused.

'Except the Dry-Mouths!'

As Polly and Tom watched Digby rehearse his performance as the Grand Fizzler, one thing became clear. He was still doing exactly as he was told. Obviously Digby the Defiant, Digby the Determined and Digby the Indestructible were still locked in his past, unable to help free him from the control of Kruud and his associates.

As the Grand Fizzler continued to rant and rave about Dry-Mouths – stopping occasionally to practise different facial expressions intended to make him look sincere, or wise, or protective, or angry – Scarlett described what she had observed over the past two nights.

'About a dozen bamboo-masters have been laying markers on the other side of the cliff for helicopters to land. They've been building special platforms for television cameras there, too, so obviously they're planning a big announcement. I wouldn't be surprised if, by this time tomorrow, every television company in the world is here to film it. What I can't work out is why they're going to all this bother, if the Grand Fizzler's just going to give us the same old nonsense about not trusting Dry-Mouths. The trouble is that he only practises snippets of the speech, so I don't know how it ends.'

Polly and Tom looked at each other.

'Badly,' said Polly.

The Dolphin with Three Tails

Tom stood on the edge of the cliff with Scarlett's parachute strapped securely to his back. In a few seconds the sun would rise over the mountain behind him and it would be light enough for him to jump. During the night he and Polly and Scarlett had decided that Tom should leave and seek help. Handing themselves over to Kruud and his bamboo-masters was out of the question, and the walk back through the mountains would take them at least two days. Scarlett was by now so exhausted and weak with hunger that Tom feared she might not survive the journey. Besides, they had to stop the Grand Fizzler from making his announcement that night. Tom would have to go alone, and the quickest way back to the ocean, they had all agreed, was down.

He jumped.

As soon as he was clear of the cliff face he pulled the ripcord. The parachute jerked open and he continued his descent to the ice, steering towards the centre where Scarlett had cut the hole a week before. Halfway down he spotted it, small but unmistakable in the vastness, like a dark-blue tiddlywink sitting in the middle of a white marble floor. As he adjusted his course he saw something moving towards it across the ice, something lumbering and white. The polar bear. Despite the cold Tom felt suddenly hot and prickly, as he realised that the huge beast was going to reach the hole before him. His heart began to pound. He wouldn't have time to land properly. There was only one thing he could do. He looked down, fifty feet, forty, thirty . . . And then he was directly above the hole, twenty feet up. He would have to judge his fall perfectly. A foot too far in either direction and he would hit the ice, a ready meal dropping out of the sky for a grateful polar bear. Now! He punched the parachute harness and raised his arms allowing himself to slip out of it. Then he tucked his arms tight into his side as he dropped towards the hole. But he hadn't allowed for the wind pushing him off target. Halfway down a sudden gust blew him sideways. Disaster. Instinctively, he bent his knees ready to crash on to the ice. Instead, the ice around the hole melted, instantly opening wide like a hungry mouth to swallow him whole. As the bear's claws sliced through the air inches away from his nose, Tom plummeted into the freezing water.

The cold took his breath away, as though every part of his body had been punched at the same time. But, as billions of tiny Fizzle bubbles clung to his body to form an invisible barrier between him and the cold, and a larger bubble formed around his head allowing him to breathe, so a degree of warmth and feeling returned to his skin. Suddenly, the face of the polar bear appeared behind him. Hungry and desperate, it had plunged in after him, its nostrils closed against the onrushing water, its ears pressed flat and streamlined against the side of its head, its broad front paws like paddles, pulling it closer and closer to its prey.

Tom turned and began to push himself through the water as fast as he could. But he knew he couldn't outswim his ravenous pursuer. If only an even faster creature would come to his rescue and guide him out of the lake . . . The Pixelfish would know the way out, of course – this was their home and they'd know exactly where the door was. But he needed to move through the water fast. The polar bear was almost on him now. He imagined a dolphin coming to his rescue, but surely not even the swiftest of them could reach him now. Unless . . .

Suddenly there it was, slicing through the water towards him, drawing a line of silvery bubbles behind it like a jet trail. And no wonder, for Tom had imagined no ordinary dolphin. It had not one tail fin but three, splayed out like propeller blades, spinning together in a foaming, silvery blur to push it through the water like a torpedo. As it passed within reach of the polar bear the animal struck out, slicing a great gouge in the dolphin's side with its claws. But the vast army of Pixelfish from which it was made reformed around the wound, healing it instantly as the dolphin continued on its way. As it passed beneath him Tom grabbed its fin. Then, with the polar bear's claws scything towards his ankles he was catapulted away, and he and the dolphin left the bear behind in a cloud of bubbles.

Once out of the bear's reach the dolphin adjusted its course and accelerated. Seconds later, the wall of the lake loomed dark and sheer in front of them. There seemed no way through it, but the dolphin continued on. Should he let go? No. He would trust the Fizzle. As they were about to hit the rock wall Tom closed his eyes.

'Aaaaaargh!'

But there was no collision. Instead, as they hit what looked like solid rock, the thin layer of Pixelfish which had assumed its shape and colour dissolved, and they passed through it as easily as a plane flying through light cloud.

Inside the tunnel the dolphin slowed down, as the water seemed suddenly to become thicker. Tom would have expected the tunnel to be dark. Instead, it glowed, as though he had been plunged into a luminous glitter storm. Holding on tight with one hand, he held out the other, watching the billions of Pixelfish light up as they sped through his fingers, illuminated by his thoughts. At the same time tiny trails of bubbles rose from them like silver threads, as they went about their day's work filtering the seawater, and turning it into Fizzle. As they sped under the mountains towards the ocean Tom noted that the passage was wide enough to accommodate the submarine which he and Polly had tried to follow. At least now he knew how the Grand Fizzler came to be under the ice.

Suddenly, far ahead, he saw the other end of the tunnel. Again, it was blocked by Pixelfish, their rocky disguise as thin as his cotton school shirt, allowing seawater to filter through, yet convincing enough to deter any predators from straying into it. He knew the Pixelfish would disperse as he reached the exit and tried to keep his eyes open. But he couldn't. At the moment of impact he closed them, only to open them a split second later to find himself back in the ocean, streaking beneath a ceiling of blurry blue ice.

The dolphin travelled faster now, picking up speed until, suddenly, it surged upwards towards a gap in the ice. When its nose broke the surface it stopped abruptly, so that Tom continued on, flying out of the water and on to the ice sheet like a penguin returning from a fishing trip. He managed to land on his feet, then watched as the dolphin dissolved back into the ocean like a sandcastle washed away by the tide. Then he turned, craning his neck to gaze up at the wall of gleaming white which towered over him. But this was no iceberg. The dolphin, or rather the Pixelfish, had brought him to the side of Kruud's yacht. Large slabs of ice floated around it like crazy paving. The largest, on which Tom stood, was being used as a jetty, connected to the yacht by a wooden gangplank which led up into its side. Bobbing gently on one side of the jetty, moored to a metal spike driven deep into the ice, was Slugbucket's caravan. The door was open, revealing it to be empty. On the other side of the ice, secured between a dozen amphibious snowmobiles, was a large golden droplet.

Similar in shape to the crystal pendant worn by the Grand Fizzler, it was about twice Tom's height and, judging by the circular hatch in its side, designed to carry passengers, no doubt in some luxury. A row of small, coloured-glass portholes were studded around its golden exterior which, in turn, was attached to a pair of gold-coloured floats that supported it on top of the water. Tom watched as the hook which had just lowered the droplet to the ocean returned slowly on the end of its chain to the crane on the yacht's main deck. Then, a few moments later, the hatch in the side of the yacht clunked open, and heavy footsteps began to bounce down the gangplank. Tom darted underneath it, then moved as close as he could to the point at which it touched the ice – the only place dark enough for him to crouch unseen. Not daring to look out, he counted footsteps instead, trying to calculate the number of people rattling the wooden planks just inches above his head. A dozen at least, maybe more. One by one, the snowmobiles' engines spluttered into life, filling the air with noise and blue-grey fumes. Then, as though a starting pistol had been fired, they roared in unison, and the convoy raced off.

Tom peeked out from his hiding place to see that six of the amphibious snowmobiles, each ridden by a fur-clad bamboo-master, were pulling the golden droplet like a carriage across the ocean. Six more – three each side of it – completed the formation, skating with equal ease over water and ice alike, as the procession sped majestically towards the shore.

'Mr Kruud always was a show-off,' thought Tom.

A few minutes later the carriage slid effortlessly from ocean to land and stopped, briefly, whilst two of the riders abandoned their snowmobiles and climbed on to the back. Then, as they clung to the gold handles protruding from it like footmen standing behind a royal coach, the carriage resumed its journey.

As the sound of the snowmobiles' engines faded Tom emerged from beneath the gangplank and climbed on board the vast, luxurious yacht. Inside, he moved quietly down the corridor leading to the main ballroom where, less than a year before, he and his crewmates had joined Mr Kruud for dinner and – between mouthfuls of soggy Alphabetiburgers and sickly-sweet Kola – told him about the Fizzle. Then, the huge room had been dominated by a giant meringue, floating like an iceberg in the centre of a large raised pool brimming with milk. Now, as Tom opened the double doors he could see that the milk and meringue had gone. But the pool remained. And it was by no means empty. He craned his neck at the millions of coins and banknotes – collected from the Grand Fizzler's devoted followers around the world – which rose towards the ceiling three storeys above like a vast money-mountain.

Positioned around the pool were a dozen large printed screens depicting the Grand Fizzler in wise and thoughtful poses. All of them had been fitted with castors allowing them to be moved around to create separate areas. Behind one of them Tom discovered a fully equipped television studio, complete with painted backgrounds which hung from the ceiling like stage scenery. They depicted such things as silver rainfall and glittering rainbows, and Tom recognised them from some of the Grand Fizzler posters that he and Polly had seen in Shipley. Hanging from one of the television cameras was an ordinary plastic bubble-making machine. Tom flipped the switch and hundreds of plain soapy bubbles began to spew out across the studio.

'I might have known they were fake, too,' he thought, turning the machine off. 'Only Seymour knows how to make real Fizzle bubbles.'

In the area beyond this he found a changing room, complete with dressing table and mirror, where no doubt Digby transformed himself into the Grand Fizzler ready for the cameras. And beyond that a dozen more tables, each of which groaned under the weight of the Grand Fizzler's printed speeches, and the towering stacks of newspapers and magazines in which all of his radio, television and personal appearances had been reported.

So . . . Tom had found it. The worldwide headquarters of KPRC Industries. The place where Kruud and his associates had masterminded the whole Grand Fizzler con trick. And it explained why he, and Punjabootee, and Robovich, and Ching had never been found, and why the Grand Fizzler appeared so mysterious and elusive. Tom sniffed the air. A faint, but familiar, smell had drifted into his nostrils. He closed his eyes to concentrate. A bit fishy perhaps . . .

Lastly, as he completed his circuit of the room he came across a collection of glass cabinets. Arranged in rows like exhibits in a museum, they displayed the full range of Grand Fizzler products – everything from the crystal pendants that filled every high-street shop and hung around the necks of people like Mr Tutt to a talking doll of the great man himself. Tom lifted one out of its cabinet and pulled the string protruding from its back.

'Have *you* got the Fizzle?' it squawked.

'*Arf!*' came the unexpected reply, as something cold and wet nudged the back of Tom's leg.

Tom nearly jumped out of his skin. He spun around, dropping the doll, which continued to talk despite landing face down on the floor.

Kruud's pet seal Arthur had shuffled quietly into the room and crept up behind him. That explained the slightly fishy smell. For some reason Tom had a sudden, seal-like craving for a tasty piece of fresh haddock. Interesting . . . He bent down and looked into the seal's large saucery eyes.

'Did you get a whiff of the Fizzle gas at the same time as Digby by any chance?'

'Arf!' barked Arthur.

'So, perhaps you know that I'm looking for my friends?' Tom continued, hopefully.

'Arf,' the seal replied, turning to shuffle out of the ballroom.

Tom followed him into the corridor and down the long red carpet which led back to the gangplank. Halfway along, the seal stopped beside a small doorway, set discreetly into the oak-panelled wall.

Tom twisted the brass handle and it clicked open. He peered inside . . .

'Are they in here?' he asked, only to see the seal's tail disappear down the gangplank in search of breakfast.

Tom turned and stepped through the doorway. In front of him, a staircase zigzagged down through the centre of the ship, with more doorways at each zig and each zag, each leading on to another deck, with more doors and more staircases. He was sure that the Captain and his other shipmates were aboard somewhere. But where should he start looking? Should he call out for them? What if there were other bamboo-masters on board, or Kruud himself? He would take the chance – perhaps from halfway down, where his voice might carry further. He skipped quickly and quietly down the stairs until he was midway. Then he stopped, and was about to shout the Captain's name, when he heard a sound – like a slow tick. So he continued on. As he followed the staircase down, the sound grew louder, its rhythm reminding him of the steady thud of Slugbucket chopping logs with his axe on the Shipley Manor estate. Closer still and it became not just louder but sharper, like red-hot iron being hammered into shape on a blacksmith's anvil. The sound led him to the bottom of the staircase where a reinforced metal hatch – locked tight by a heavy lever – barred his way. Tom's heart was pounding. He was alone, and whoever, or whatever, was behind the door was clearly striking something with brute force.

'Captain,' he called, doubtful that his voice would penetrate the thick steel separating him from the inside. 'Captain, are you there?'

There was no reply. He would have to open the door. He put his hands on the lever to lift it. As he did so, the sound inside stopped.

Attack of the Ice Arrows

Moolah's hands were red-raw. She tore two more strips of cloth from her vest and wrapped them around her blistered and bleeding fingers before returning to her task, hacking away at the ice with the Captain's sword. After nearly a day she was almost there, even though each blow scarcely scratched its surface. But a few more strikes and the block of ice in which the Captain had been encased would split in half and he would be free. Only then would she discover whether he was alive or dead.

The attack had come from an unexpected source. She, the Captain, Slugbucket and Mr Grub had boarded Kruud's yacht the day before. It had appeared deserted, so they had begun searching for the Grand Fizzler, or Kruud, or anyone who might know of Scarlett's whereabouts. Aware too that she and Kruud were old enemies, the Captain was determined to search every cabin and cubby-hole for her, in case she was being held captive. After an hour they had reached the belly of the yacht, and stepped through the hatch into Kruud's wine store which lay on the other side. The room was long and wide, made narrower by the rows of huge wooden barrels which lay on their sides along both walls, and the thousands of bottles stacked above them, their corks aimed across the divide like the artillery of two opposing armies waiting to open fire. Moolah – who as one of Kruud's bamboo-masters had been on the yacht many times – knew that at the far end of the room another hatch led into the yacht's cargo hold, the one place they hadn't searched. Having noticed that the yacht lay low in the water the Captain suspected that the hold must be full. But of what? They had decided to find out and, at the same time, check that Scarlett wasn't being held prisoner there.

They'd barely taken a step forward when the artillery had opened fire. Only the corks that had started to fly didn't come from bottles of wine. The bottles, and the barrels below them, contained Kruud's private hoard of Fizzle. As they stepped towards the cargo hold the barrels nearest to them exploded, whilst corks flew and Fizzle burst out of the bottles in long gushing jets which began to freeze the moment they touched the air. Instantly, they had become engulfed in water, freezing them midstep. Only Moolah had escaped, launching herself upwards to cling on to the metal grille covering one of the ceiling lights which ran down the centre of the room. Then, moments later, the deluge had stopped and she had looked down at her companions, encased in huge jagged explosions of ice. Immediately around her the Fizzle bottles dripped empty, whilst the barrels' shattered planks lay strewn over the floor like driftwood on an icy sea. And she had lowered herself down. Then she heard a noise behind her, turning just as Luka, the bamboo-master who had always hated her, slammed the hatch shut and locked them in.

After that there had been only one way to go – forward. She had attempted to reach the other end and make her way into the cargo hold, there perhaps to find some way of releasing her companions and herself, but the Fizzle would not let her pass. Any attempt was met with further explosions which threatened to freeze her to the spot, whilst jets of Fizzle arced down from the shelves above, freezing like thick prison bars in front of her, blocking her path. She could find no way through. And then she had noticed the handle of the Captain's sword protruding from the block of ice in which he was frozen, and had begun the long task of freeing him. Now, having worked all night and ripped several layers of skin from her fingers, she was nearly there, just a few more blows with the sword . . .

Suddenly the door had squeaked. She jumped up, wrapping her fingers around the lighting grille, her feet pressed tight against the ceiling, the Captain's heavy sword clamped between her teeth. As soon as the figure walked through the hatchway she dropped down on to his back, pushing him to the floor. Aaaargh! Then in a flash she was up, her foot pressed hard on Tom's spine, the point of the Captain's sword pricking the back of his neck.

'Tom?'

As she withdrew the sword he turned around and sat up, rubbing his neck, full of questions.

But Moolah had a job to finish and had already returned to the Captain. She raised the sword above his head.

'Noooooo!' Tom cried, but he was too late. He closed his eyes as the sword swung down with a mighty crack, splitting the ice block in half like a chopped log. As the two halves fell apart Moolah caught the Captain as his knees buckled. For a moment he seemed unsteady on his feet, as though he had woken from a deep sleep.

'Your skin is still warm,' Moolah observed, releasing his hand.

The Captain took out his pocket watch. A clock above the hatchway leading into the cargo hold confirmed that time had continued to move on, even though he hadn't.

'But . . . I don't understand.'

'You've been trapped in the ice since yesterday,' Moolah explained. 'The Fizzle stopped us from reaching the cargo hold.'

'Really?' said the Captain. 'Why in the Seven Seas would it do that, I wonder?'

He prised the sword gently from Moolah's sticky red fingers.

'Perhaps I'd better free the other two,' he said, before stepping over to Slugbucket, who had been frozen between two barrages of ice. He raised the sword above his head, then brought the blade down with a steely swish. The ice around Slugbucket cracked open like an eggshell, and he stumbled forward on to his knees.

'Are you all right, Slugbucket?' asked Tom.

'S'pose so,' he mumbled, spitting a large chunk of ice out of his mouth. 'The last thing oi remember is gettin' a mouthful o' Fizzle. Then it must 'a frozen. Funny though . . . you'd think I'd 'ave one o' them ice-cream 'eadaches, wouldn't you?'

Then it was Grub's turn. He was frozen in a crouch, having stretched his dark, baggy overcoat over his head in a failed attempt to protect himself. With another swift stroke from the Captain's blade he was free. As the ice fell away Grub peeked out from under his coat, only emerging once he had spotted the Captain's boots.

The Captain returned his sword to its sheath and looked around him. Then he turned to Tom.

'Where's Polly?'

'She's safe –' Tom swallowed hard. '– by the lake with Scarlett.'

The Captain's eyes widened. He had no idea what had happened. But he did know what was most important. He turned his back on the cargo hold and put a hand on Tom's shoulder.

'In that case let's go and get them, shipmate. Lead the way.'

But Tom hesitated.

'Something really bad is going to happen, Captain. Something we have to stop. I told Polly and Scarlett that I'd search the whole yacht for clues before going back for them.'

The Captain glanced back at the cargo hold.

'They made me promise,' Tom insisted.

The Captain paced back and forth for a few seconds, rubbing his chin which, by now, had grown quite stubbly.

'All right,' he said, drawing out his sword again. 'Only this time we won't be taken by surprise.'

He pushed the tip of his sword into a plank from one of the broken barrels and lifted it up. 'Mr Grub, I want you to wedge the hatch open with this, then make your way back to the gangplank and keep watch. If you see any of those scoundrels heading back this way, return here as quickly as you can to warn us.'

Grub clicked his heels and saluted, before turning to waddle back to the open hatch.

Once he had gone, the Captain surveyed the battlefield.

Ahead of them, at the end of the long room, was the door that they needed to reach. In between lay thousands more gallons of the Fizzle, which seemed intent on stopping them. The barrels which had already burst open were in splinters, except for two, whose round lids had blown off whole. Each taller than Tom, they lay among the debris of battle like two wooden shields abandoned by retreating giants. The Captain examined one of them.

'Shipmates,' he said, 'I have an idea.'

A few minutes later they had heaved both lids on to their rims so that they stood upright, like two enormous wheels. The planks on the outside of the wheels facing the Fizzle were smooth. On the inside, though, several struts ran across holding them all together. These made perfect handholds, and would allow them to grip and turn the wheels as they walked between them, shielding them from the Fizzle on either side. Slugbucket would turn one, and Tom and Moolah the other. They manoeuvred themselves into position between the wheels, then the Captain stepped in front to lead the way, only his sword protruding forward beyond the protection of the wood. Finally, having tilted both wheels together at the top like a letter A to protect them from aerial attack, they were ready.

'Steady as she goes then, shipmates,' said the Captain. 'Start rolling.'

Slowly, Slugbucket, Moolah and Tom began to roll the wheels forward, keeping their heads and bodies tucked close to the wood. Careful not to step too far ahead, the Captain began to hack through the ice which had previously blocked Moolah's path. For a moment they thought the Fizzle might allow them to reach the door. But they were wrong. Suddenly it opened fire. Barrels on both sides exploded open, sending water crashing against the sides, pushing the wheels closer together. The wheels remained upright but had become suddenly heavier as a thick coating of ice clung to the outside, threatening to weld them to the ground.

'Keep moving,' the Captain ordered as another barrel exploded, this time knocking Tom over. He picked himself up and returned to the wheel as Moolah kept it rolling forward. Suddenly the sound of gunfire echoed around the cellar as a thousand Fizzle bottles popped their corks and sent jets of water streaking in their direction, freezing into spears which thudded against the sides of the shields, some with such force that they stuck into the wood. At the front, the Captain hacked away with his sword as Fizzle streaked down ahead of them, forming frozen prison bars to block their path. Above them, some of the Fizzle managed to get through, falling like heavy showers on their heads and shoulders, soaking into their clothes before freezing, threatening to set their clothes like concrete if they paused for breath.

'Keep moving,' the Captain repeated. 'We *must* keep moving.'

Suddenly, another barrel exploded, knocking Moolah and Tom and the Captain over with the heavy lid on top of them. Slugbucket was exposed. He turned, helpless, as a hundred bottles opened fire. In a split second the jets of Fizzle had turned to ice. He backed against the wheel as they sliced through the air, closing his eyes as dozens of ice-daggers slammed into the wheel around him, pinning his coat and baggy trousers to the wood as though he were a knife-thrower's assistant.

'Oi'm gettin' a bit fed up wi' thi –' he muttered, just as the next barrel exploded and a deluge of water hit him square on, freezing against him instantly.

'Slugbucket!' cried Tom.

But his shipmate didn't reply. Instead, for a few moments, the room fell silent.

'We're over halfway,' the Captain whispered, as though the Fizzle might be listening. 'We have to keep going.'

The lid, already covered in a thick coating of ice, was too heavy to lift back up. Besides, it would only offer protection from one side. Their only hope was to carry it like a tortoise shell and crawl towards the hatch on their hands and knees. They steadied themselves on all fours, the lid pressing down on their backs, and began to crawl forward. Except the Captain.

'Blithering chilblains!' he cursed, twisting round to see that his feet – which had been sticking out from the protective cover of the wood – had become encased in blocks of ice. These, in turn, were welded solid to the floor. He was stuck.

'Take my sword and keep going,' he told Tom. 'The Fizzle won't hurt me. It just wants to stop us –' He heaved in vain to free his feet. '– and I'm well and truly stopped.'

So, Moolah and Tom began to crawl forward, gradually exposing the Captain to whatever fate the Fizzle had in store for him. Instead, it left him stuck to the floor like a stick-in-the-mud, whilst it concentrated its firepower on Tom and Moolah. Another barrel came alive, but this time it didn't explode. Instead, the wooden sides and the lid remained largely intact, forcing the Fizzle out through narrow slits between the planks. Suddenly the air was full of wafer-thin sheets of ice, spinning like razor-sharp snowflakes the size of dinner plates as they bombarded the barrel lid protecting Tom and Moolah, slicing through its icy coating before cutting great gouges in the wood in an effort to destroy their defences. As more barrels joined the assault, volleys of pencil-thin ice arrows screeched out of colander holes punched in their sides, embedding themselves in the wooden shield like the spines of an enormous hedgehog. Slowly, the planks in the shield began to fray and split until, finally, one of them was ripped out of its centre. Immediately another barrel exploded, launching a pondful of water over the top of the lid, instantly flattening Tom and Moolah against the foot-thick slab of ice which coated the floor. Tom stopped, unable to move. Fizzle had gushed through the hole in the lid, forming a solid block stretching from shoulder to knee down one side of his body, freezing him to the ground.

Suddenly there was a huge roar, as Moolah twisted on to her back and pushed the lid up with her hands and knees, before kicking it sideways and leaping to her feet. Tom watched as she hurled herself at the door, swinging the Captain's sword around her head. As another two barrels burst open either side of her she leaped up, clinging to a light grille as the two massive water bombs exploded beneath her, freezing together like a huge crystal water-lily. Then, as the racks of bottles above them erupted she dropped down, rolling forward as the two volleys of missiles collided above her, showering her with jagged, frozen shards. With the hatchway now just a few feet away, almost all the remaining bottles burst open, and hundreds of criss-crossing water jets froze in a thick, protective tangle to block her path. Moolah continued on, wielding the sword like a machete as she hacked her way through the obstruction, sending countless bars of ice crashing to the floor until she was within arm's length of the door. As she reached for the lever the final two barrels exploded and a solid wall of Fizzle hit her body from each side, clamping all but her outstretched arm in their icy grip. Then, as she pulled the lever, still hoping to get a glimpse inside the cargo hold, the last bottle burst open and scored a direct hit on her arm, freezing it as though it were encased in plaster. The hatch remained shut. Finally, the room fell silent again, but for the ticking of the clock above the hatch. Moolah looked up, helpless inside her icy straitjacket, as the long hand approached the top to signal the passing of yet another hour.

Ten seconds.

Five.

One.

Then it clicked, and suddenly the Fizzle fell away from her body, cascading to the floor in a warm, tingling gush. The daggers holding Slugbucket, and the Captain's ice boots, and Tom's frozen shoulder all melted at the same time, and joined the rest of the Fizzle as it began to flow gently out of the doorway.

Slugbucket plucked a handful of corks from his hair and dropped them into the water.

'Oither the Fizzle can't make up its bloomin' mind . . .' he complained, watching the corks join the armada of wooden debris floating around his ankles, '. . . or it's deliberately bin wastin' our time – an' why would it do that?'

'I don't know,' replied the Captain, 'but I have no intention of wasting any more.'

As he stepped up to the hatchway Moolah returned his sword to him and stood aside. Then, the Captain lifted the lever . . . and opened the hatch.

Have You Got the Fizzle?

The cargo hold was like a warehouse several decks high, with a large hatch set into the ceiling through which goods could be raised and lowered. Rows of crates and boxes, piled high in long, towering stacks, stretched the length of the hold to create four aisles between them.

'Let's search an aisle each,' the Captain suggested, disappearing between two high stacks of cardboard boxes. The other shipmates set off to investigate. Tom took the first aisle, either side of which rose piles of wooden crates, stacked like interlocking bricks so that they wouldn't topple over. He was looking around for something with which to prise one open when he heard the unmistakable swish of the Captain's sword, followed by a low, painful moan. He ran back to find the Captain, head bowed, his sword hanging limp at his side. Moolah joined them, the fruits of her search – a dozen crystal pendants – strung around her neck.

'There are millions of them,' she told Tom, 'and the price has gone up, look.'

Tom lifted one of the pendants, on which hung a small price tag with a huge price printed on it.

'That's the cost of a house!' he said, his eyes wide in astonishment.

'Or a life,' said the Captain. 'I think you'd better take a look at these, shipmates.'

The Captain had sliced open a large cardboard box from which a dozen posters had spilled out on to the floor. It was another Grand Fizzler poster, only worse. This was the Grand Fizzler's declaration the solution to the so-called 'Dry-Mouth problem' – which Digby was about to announce to the world.

THE FIZZLE DECLARES THAT FROM THIS DAY:

1. ALL DRY-MOUTHS MUST REPORT TO THE LOCAL AUTHORITIES FOR REGISTRATION

2. ALL HOUSES, SHOPS AND FACTORIES OWNED BY DRY-MOUTHS SHALL BECOME THE PROPERTY OF KPRC INDUSTRIES

3. DRY-MOUTHS FAILING TO COMPLY WILL
BE ARRESTED

4. SHELTERING A KNOWN DRY-MOUTH IS
AN OFFENCE PUNISHABLE BY
IMPRISONMENT

5. ALL GOOD CITIZENS ARE ENTITLED TO
USE FORCE TO ENSURE THAT DRY-MOUTHS
COMPLY WITH THE ABOVE

IF YOU'VE 'GOT THE FIZZLE' YOU HAVE
NOTHING TO FEAR . . . JUST BE SURE TO
WEAR YOUR CRYSTAL PENDANT.

Beneath these words was a photograph of the Grand Fizzler, smiling, alongside his signature and the distinctive water droplet seal demonstrating the authenticity of the poster. Suddenly the anger which had slowly been turning the Captain's face crimson exploded.

'This is a declaration of war!'

'That'll explain these then, Cap'n,' said Slugbucket, reappearing with a rifle held aloft in each hand. 'Oi found them in some wooden crates back there. Looks loik there's thousands of 'em.'

Suddenly, Tom felt sick with fear – there were numerous crates like that where he'd been looking, too.

'What's going to happen to Mr Grub, and Carlos, and Mr and Mrs Bloom and their shop, and –'

'Nothing!' barked the Captain. 'Because we're not going to let it.'

He stormed towards the hatch, pausing only to bring a stray box of Grand Fizzler dolls chattering to life with a hefty kick, before striding out of the cargo hold and through the wine cellar. Then, with his shipmates trailing behind him, he began leaping up the stairs two at a time. At the top he stopped, and turned to them.

'We'll meet at the caravan in five minutes. Moolah, I want you to raid the cabins for warm clothes and blankets. Slugbucket, bring whatever rations you can find in the kitchen, and get rid of those guns please, shipmate – they make me nervous.'

'Roight y'are, Cap'n.'

The Captain turned back to Tom.

'Now then, I want to know everything that's happened.'

So, as Slugbucket and Moolah set off in search of supplies, Tom told the Captain about Digby and the television cameras, and about how the Grand Fizzler was due to make his announcement as soon as the light faded. The Captain fished out his pocket watch. Time was running out. They were well inside the Arctic Circle and darkness would fall again in a couple of hours. They would have to act swiftly. The Captain's plan was simple. Once Polly and Scarlett were safe he would invite the world's press to see the Grand Fizzler's floating headquarters. He would reveal the fakery that he and his shipmates had discovered. He would show them the vast money mountain and send it toppling so that they could hear for themselves the sound of Kruud's greed. He would take them to see the secret hoard of Fizzle – or what remained of it – which Kruud and his associates had no intention of sharing out. And if the reporters wouldn't come, he would make them. He would drag them on board – kicking and screaming if he had to – to witness what the world needed to know.

Back in the main corridor they found Grub hunched and shivering at the top of the gangplank, staring at the worn-out picture of Venetia Pike, protected from the icy wind by his hand. He stood up, stiffly, as if to attention. The Captain put a hand on his shoulder.

'We're off to find Polly and Scarlett, old chap,' he said, looking down at the jetty. 'The caravan won't be big enough for all of us. I want you to stay here. If anyone turns up, find a hiding place and don't move from it. We'll come back for you.'

Grub nodded. Then Moolah and Slugbucket

bustled through the door, loaded with food and blankets, and the four of them set off down the gangplank. Grub watched from the top as, two minutes later, Tom reeled in the mooring rope and the caravan began chugging slowly towards the shore. With Slugbucket steering the small red outboard motor at the back, Tom joined the Captain and Moolah on the caravan's front steps, guiding them towards the two snowmobiles which he had seen abandoned earlier that day. At the same time he continued telling them everything he knew about Digby and his speech. The Captain was barely able to contain his puffing, blustering outrage. But Moolah remained silent, her head bowed in shame.

'What's wrong?' asked Tom.

'Digby,' she replied. 'I made his life a misery on Dollar Island. He must hate me.'

As the caravan neared the shore, its wheels finally touched the ground and the engine, with one last surge, sent it rolling clear of the water. The snowmobiles were still there, standing amid numerous tracks in the snow, all of which led up the long slope towards the gap in the mountains. The Captain pressed his boot into the whiteness. Good – it was quite firm. Their progress would be slow, but at least they shouldn't get stuck.

The Mystery of the Missing Pebbles

Polly put down the ice saw and admired her handiwork. The cave was a bit rough and ready, but it would do. With the parachute gone she and Scarlett had become exposed, their shelter no longer camouflaged against the snow. So she had taken the ice saw and found a large snowdrift close to the edge of the woods. There she had hollowed out a space big enough for them to hide in, but with an entrance no wider than their shoulders. From their new base she would be able to listen out for Tom and watch developments as they unfolded around the cliff edge. Scarlett, meanwhile, needed to rest and prepare for the journey back. Having survived for the past two days on nothing but a handful of toffees she was too weak to walk far. They would have to wait for

Tom and the Captain.

Polly lay quietly, peeping out like a rabbit from its warren, as the sun set, pushed aside by a crisp moon which sliced through the trees to cast black and blue zebra stripes across the snow. Suddenly, the sky was full of sound and light as helicopters roared overhead, their searchlights criss-crossing the ground as they located their landing markers on the other side of the lake. These were the Grand Fizzler's guests, invited to the home of the Fizzle which – His Effervescence had assured them – was about to make an important declaration. As the helicopters landed in a kaleidoscope of light and swirling snow, and their crews began to set up the television cameras with which they would broadcast the announcement to the world, Polly tied on her snowshoes and wiggled out of the shelter. Keeping to the shadows she made her way to the edge of the wood and looked out. A dozen bamboo-masters were clustered around the cliff edge watching the helicopters land on the far side. In between, stationary amid the abandoned snowmobiles which had pulled it there, was something which looked like a giant water droplet balanced between two long floats. From the hatch in the side Polly guessed that it was some kind of carriage. But who was inside?

The bamboo-masters were standing with their

backs to her. If she was very quiet perhaps she could sneak a look inside. Perhaps the carriage was empty. Perhaps there might be food and blankets which she could take back for Scarlett. Even if she was spotted, the bamboo-masters were some distance away. For Scarlett's sake she had to risk it. She crept forward, and stepped on to one of the floats. As she reached for the hatch she looked over her shoulder to check that the bamboo-masters' attention was still elsewhere. When she turned back the hatch was open. Before she could escape a hand shot out, gripping her wrist and snatching her inside. Then the hatch clunked shut behind her.

'Ssssscream all you like, ssssweetie,' said Venetia Pike, glaring at her from across a small round table. 'No one can hear you.'

But Polly didn't say a word. She shrank back into the seat into which she'd been thrown, as far as possible from the foul, fishy breath of her captor. The carriage was lined with padded leather, bright pink to match the deep, luxurious upholstery of the seating. Beneath her pink fur hat Pike was wrapped in a full-length pink fur coat and matching mittens. The stiletto heels on her red snakeskin boots were sunk deep into a white rug covering the floor. Polly leaned forward to run her fingers through the fur.

'Baby polar bear,' Pike explained with a cruel

smile. 'I always do my best to use local produce.'

Polly recoiled into her seat and looked across at Pike who, despite being swathed in thick fur, looked anything but cuddly.

'We thought you were dead,' she said.

'You should know better than that,' Pike replied. 'It's true that your friend stole the flying skills I'd, er, inherited from Hopper Hawkins just as I was using them to fly Sherman H. Kruud's rather sssplendid jet. So, for a few moments I did lose control. But at the same time – just before Dollar Island exploded – Sherman and his friends breathed in the Fizzle gas whilst sitting inside that giant contraption of theirs. I couldn't have timed it better myself. Before you could say "Cobra Candelabra", I'd nipped into Sherman's mind and taken his flying skills instead. They're not a patch on the old man's, of course, but beggars can't be choosers, especially when you're plummeting to earth in a plane that you have no idea how to fly.'

Pike smiled. 'That's the second time the Fizzle has saved me, you know,' she said, leaning forward to tap Polly's knee menacingly with her fingernail. 'I think it rather likessss me.'

'Where are Mr Kruud and the others now?' asked Polly.

Pike sat back in her seat and wafted her hand casually in the air.

'Oh, they're . . . around . . .'

Polly looked bemused. Suddenly Pike threw her head back and laughed.

'Fool! They're here, right in front of you.' She took off one of her mittens and retrieved something from her pocket. Then, she held her upturned fist over the table . . . and opened it.

'My pebbles!'

'That's right. The Fizzle didn't kill Kruud and his friends. It just . . . squashed them up a bit. Reduced them to rubble, you might say. But not before they'd become Fizzlers, albeit of a far inferior quality to me, of course. And since I retrieved them from your bedroom a few months ago they've been exactly where I want them – in the palm of my hand. You see, even though their bodies might be a little . . . incapacitated, their minds, however feeble, are still alive. So I can hold silent conversations with Sherman and his stony associates just like you can with Tom. And they've been sssso co-operative. When I threatened to drop them into the nearest rock grinder they gave me the numbers of their ssssecret bank accounts –' She clicked her fingers. '– just like that! And when I suggested drilling holes through them to make a nice pebble necklace they almost begged me to take control of their business empires. So you see, I own KPRC Industries, not them. Not that Digby the Dimwit has a clue about any of this of course. He's confined to the submarine unless he's needed on board the yacht to sit in front of a camera, and then he only ever sees bamboo-masters. The ssssilly old fool just thinks that his boss is away on business the whole time. He has no idea that he, and Sherman and his friends, and the whole delicioussssly ssstupid world are all dancing to *my* tune. And you know what sort of dance it will be after tonight, don't you, sssweetie?' She leant over and whispered in Polly's ear. 'A war dance!'

Slowly, she wrapped her long, spidery fingers around the pebbles, and held them up in front of Polly.

'And, of course, whenever any of them start ssssslacking – well, you'd be surprised what can be achieved by banging a few heads together.' Suddenly, she shook her fist, and the sound of a rattlesnake shaking its tail filled the carriage. Now, Polly understood why Kruud and his associates fell to their knees clutching their heads, whenever they heard it. Pike – the phantom rattler – was rattling *them*.

Demonstration over, Pike let the pebbles fall with a clatter on to the table. Polly winced.

'Oh, I wouldn't feel too sorry for them,' said Pike, 'especially Sherman. At least he still has the pleasure of tormenting his old manservant – not that Digby's much of a man, of course. He's more of a timid little mouse really, isn't he?'

Pike looked at her watch. Good, the show was about to start. She stood up and began fiddling with the television which hung from the centre of the domed ceiling.

'Come on, you stupid ssssquare-faced goggle-box!'

She thumped it hard on the side and the screen flickered into life. Then, she sat back down, beckoning Polly over with the curl of a talon.

'Sit next to me, ssssweetie, away from the hatch. I want you to watch Digby ssssqueak for his supper.'

Suddenly, as Polly joined Pike in front of the television she had an idea.

As the face of the Grand Fizzler filled the screen and Pike dimmed the lights to watch his performance, Polly screwed her eyes up tight and began counting backwards. She had a message for Digby.

The Pocket Locksmith

In the glass observation bubble on top of the submarine Digby peered through the semi-darkness at his watch. It was almost time for his big performance. He had straightened his crystal pendant and adjusted his Grand Fizzler costume, then tilted his reclining chair backwards so that he was facing the surface of the lake a few hundred feet above him. Very soon he would switch on the lights and his bearded face would be projected a mile wide across the ice. Across the world billions of people would witness the extraordinary spectacle, and listen to the declaration which he didn't want to make. He knew it was wrong. But what choice did he have?

That was on the outside, in the real world. But in his mind, the true Digby stood in his butler's uniform, staring at the attic mirror. His

Effervescence the Grand Fizzler stared back at him from the glass, ready to begin his speech. Digby's job was to prompt him if he forgot his lines, and to guide his every gesture and movement like a maestro conducting an orchestra, so that the Grand Fizzler gave the performance of his life.

'Don't forget – nice an' loud, with plenty of anger an' fake sincerity,' Kruud had instructed him. 'An' remember what we'll do if it ain't convincin'.'

Digby knew that if the Grand Fizzler didn't perform well there would be an unbearable price to pay. Kruud and the others would destroy even more of his precious memories: his first day at school, the times he went fishing with his father – all the things that made him warm and comfortable when he remembered them. They wouldn't hesitate. Because, if he failed to follow their instructions, the rattling would begin. They would clutch their heads, rolling on the ground in agony until the noise stopped. And then, in turn, they would punish him even more severely. He wished they would just disappear. But wishing wasn't enough. He would have to kick them out of his mind himself. Only then would he be able to say, and do, and think what he wanted. But he wasn't strong enough. If he could summon strength from the brave and courageous Digbys of his childhood then, perhaps, he might succeed. But they were locked away in his past, and he had no idea how to release them.

He looked in the mirror. His Effervescence had begun talking. Having rehearsed the speech a hundred times his words tumbled out fluently, leaving Digby with little to do except watch, and listen as the Grand Fizzler's voice grew steadily louder, and more insistent.

And then he heard another voice. Much quieter, like a whisper but all around him, as though it were coming from the walls, and the floor, and the forest, and the sky all at the same time. It belonged to the girl who had spoken to him earlier. Polly.

'You *do* have a key!' she was whispering. 'The key mouse can unlock your past, Digby – I bet it can unlock anything!'

Digby looked down into his breast pocket. As if it had been waiting for his call the mouse poked its head out. As his reflection continued with the speech, Digby sneaked out of the attic, out of the tree house and out of the forest. He made his way down to the foyer of the Grand Hotel and peeled back an ancient Chinese rug from the floor. Underneath it was a trapdoor. He opened it and climbed through, replacing the rug as best he could before closing the door behind him.

He lowered himself down the metal ladder inside and on to a circular walkway. The surrounding wall at the top was made of freshly laid stone, unblemished but for the barrage of cruel, thoughtless words gouged deep into its surface – insults hurled at him by Mr Kruud day after day, week after week for as long as he could remember. Banisters ran around the inside of the walkway, before plunging down as they followed the spiral staircase leading down from it. Digby looked over the banister, peering into the gloom as if he were trying, unsuccessfully, to see the bottom of a very deep well. He stroked the mouse.

'Well, I suppose my childhood was rather a long time ago,' he explained.

He began his descent, gripping the banister nervously as it led him down into his past. The deeper he travelled the darker and more weathered the stones in the surrounding wall became, the more the black paint on the metal staircase cracked and peeled away to make way for rust. But as Digby's memory of long ago dimmed and the light with it, the cruel, mocking words remained constant, following him down, their damp, mould-filled letters festering in the dark stonework.

Half-wit
Dim-wit
Dung-breath
Nit-wit
Pea-brain
Bird-brain
Numbskull
No-brain
Gormless
Witless
Clumsy
Useless
Fathead
Thickhead
Stupid
Pinhead
Brainless
Dumbass
Doormat
Jackass

He tried to ignore them, but each one whispered
to him from the wall as he passed, hitting him like a

punch in the stomach, weakening him, slowing him down and, ultimately, convincing him of his own worthlessness. Gradually, the staircase became a spiral of despair, each step draining Digby of hope so that by the time he reached the bottom his arms hung limp at his side, and he could barely drag one foot in front of the other. Wearily, he lifted his head. In front of him was a door across which a single word had been painted in huge dripping letters. The word shone out in the semi-darkness, all the better to deliver its knockout punch.

'Loser', it said.

Digby slumped back against the wall, then sank slowly to the floor, his head bowed forward so that his chin rested on his chest. Of course he was a loser. Kruud had told him so often enough. He would never be able to stand up to him. What a fool he'd been ever to think that he could. He rested for a few moments then dragged himself back on to his feet. He would go back. If he was lucky Mr Kruud might not have noticed that he'd gone. Gently, he patted his pocket.

'Sorry to have wasted your time, little mouse,' he said.

But the pocket was empty. Slowly, he turned back to the door. The silver key mouse was there, its tiny claws wrapped around the handle as it hung upside down, sniffing the keyhole below. Then, before he could retrieve it the mouse turned itself around and thrust its long wiry tail inside. After some bottom wiggling and a few squeaks of mousy exertion, Digby heard a sharp 'click', and the little locksmith climbed back on to the door handle. Digby held out his hand and it leaped on to his sleeve, pausing to brush its whiskers before diving into his shirt pocket. He hesitated for a moment. Then, trembling, he turned the handle and the door creaked open.

Inside was dark and still, but not empty. It was full of sound: the trickle of distant laughter, the creaking of swings in the park, the crash of waves tumbling on to summer shores. He closed his eyes, listening to his childhood. Remembering. Then, another sound began to grow in the darkness. A pair of lone footsteps, walking towards him. But they weren't alone for long. Soon others joined them, then more. And as their numbers multiplied so they began to run, slowly at first, then faster and faster until their pounding feet began to shake the ground. Digby pressed himself back against the wall, as though at any moment a herd of cattle might burst through the doorway and trample him. And not a moment too soon. Suddenly, as the rumble became a roar the door was thrown back, and dozens of boys stampeded out of Digby's past. Pushing him aside they thundered up the staircase – defiant Digbys, daring Digbys, brave and determined Digbys – sending clouds of rust-red dust cascading down through its centre as they leaped up the steps two at a time to reclaim the mind that was rightly theirs.

As the dust settled Digby tried to follow them. But his own timidity held him back. And then he heard something else approaching – a familiar squeak that he hadn't heard for many years. A few seconds later, from the dimmest, most distant corner of Digby's memory, a toddler pedalled out of the darkness. No more than three years old he was riding a bicycle, bravely trying to keep up with the bigger boys. His knees were scarred and bloody from constant falls, but his face was set firm as he squeak-squeak-squeaked past Digby towards the staircase, determined to play his part. Digby the Indestructible. Ashamed that even a three-year-old was prepared to face up to Kruud when he was not, Digby took off his butler's jacket and threw it through the open doorway, into his past. Then, as he heaved the door shut he noticed that something had changed. The letters scrawled across it had begun to fade.

By now Digby the Indestructible had reached the staircase and was trying to lift the bicycle on to the first step. But it was too heavy for him. He turned to Digby, stretching out his tiny hands for help. Digby bent down to pick him up, and as he lifted him into his arms the little boy began to fade, slowly dissolving into him like a ghost. At the same time Digby began to feel braver, and stronger, and just a little bit . . . indestructible. He put the bicycle carefully to one side then, like the Digbys who had just gone before him, he ran up the steps two at a time.

All was quiet as he emerged from the trapdoor. The foyer of the Grand Hotel was deserted. The receptionist, the doorman, the liftboy, they had all disappeared the moment he threw away his jacket. Strange . . . Then he heard a quiet 'ping' and, suddenly, the boys exploded out of the lift, carrying Ching, Punjabootee and Robovich high above their heads on a sea of hands. For a second time Digby stood aside as the boys swept past him, and threw the three unwanted guests out of the building, and out of his mind. But Kruud remained somewhere inside, and as the boys stormed back into the foyer Digby barred their way.

'I have to do this by myself,' he said quietly. But they seemed not to hear. Instead, they ran straight into him, one by one disappearing in a puff of dust, like layers of time being blown from the cover of a long-forgotten book. And with each collision Digby felt stronger, and braver, and more determined until, finally, his head raised high and proud above his collar, he headed for the lift in search of Mr Kruud.

He didn't have far to look. As he stepped back into the forest, Kruud was there waiting for him.

Digby the Indestructible

'You're supposed to be up in the tree house makin' sure the Grand Fizzler don't forget his lines,' Kruud barked as Digby stepped out of the lift. The barrel of Kruud's gun was still hot and smoking. Slung over his shoulder, its thick, furry tail clasped in his fist, was a Guam flying fox. Kruud dropped it to the ground.

'I need a new set of head covers for my golf clubs,' he explained casually, reaching into his pocket for a handful of mini-meringues which he proceeded to flick, one by one, into his mouth. 'Now get back up to the attic an' do your damn job.'

But Digby didn't move. Instead, he took a deep breath. Then, he said something which he had never, ever, said to Sherman H Kruud before.

'No,' he said.

Kruud staggered back, as though suddenly a

huge invisible boxing glove had hit him in the face. For a moment he was silent. Then, his face started to swell, as blood-red rage began pumping through his body.

'It ain't up to you, boy,' he yelled, striding forward to press his nose against the butler's. 'You don't get to decide what to do. You ain't nothing but Digby the Doorman, Digby the Delivery Boy, Digby the Dumb Waiter, Digby the ditherin', dough-brained dogsbody who'll do as he's damn well told.'

He paused for a moment to catch his breath.

'An' if you don't you'll soon be Digby the *Deceased*!'

But Digby stood firm. Defiant.

'Are you listenin', boy? Or are you Digby the Deaf as well?'

'My hearing is quite all right, sir. Thank you for asking.'

'Then do as I say!'

'No,' Digby repeated, quietly. 'In fact, sir, I'm afraid I'm going to have to ask you to leave.'

Kruud's mouth dropped open, causing his hand automatically to stuff another meringue into it.

'An' who's gonna make me?' he snarled, raising his fist. 'There's more power in one of my little fingers than in your entire body, you decrepit old dinosaur.'

Digby smiled.

'That may be true in the outside world, sir,' he replied, 'but we're here, inside my mind, where I can imagine just about anything . . . including being a thousand times stronger than you. In fact,' he added, calmly wiping a spatter of meringue crumbs from his forehead, 'I could even imagine being a dinosaur if that's really what you think I am.'

'Well, you sure as hell smell as though you've been dead for a few million years,' Kruud sneered, failing entirely to recognise Digby's warning.

'So be it then, sir,' said the butler. 'I wouldn't want to disappoint you.'

Suddenly, Digby's tired, bloodshot eyes flashed bright yellow, and before Kruud could move away he found himself gripped between a set of huge claws which had sprung from Digby's sleeve. With his arms pinned to the side of his body, his shotgun fell to the ground, and Kruud could do nothing except watch as his elderly butler transformed himself into the biggest, most deadly fighting machine that nature had ever created. As Digby's eyes grew rounder, and larger, and slid slowly to the side of his face Kruud heard the sound of huge spines ripping through the back of the butler's shirt. Then the rest of his uniform was shredded into rags as Digby started to grow wider, taller, stronger. And as he grew, so Kruud was lifted from his feet, face to face with the dinosaur's huge snarling snout. As the beast flexed its muscles so Digby flexed his imagination, constantly changing shape as, like a giant medieval knight shopping for the perfect weaponry, he tried on different sets of armour plating, and alternative combinations of spikes, claws and horns with which to impale, bludgeon or smash the bones of his opponent.

Helpless in the dinosaur's grip, his feet dangling twenty feet in the air and with Digby's thumb – now a terrifying spike the size of a rhinoceros horn – pressed under his chin, Kruud was forced to look at his own terrified reflection in Digby's huge beady eye, and contemplate the moment when he would strike. Would death come as a single bite to his neck? Would his ribs be crushed like dry twigs? Or would he simply be thrashed like a rag doll against the nearest tree trunk. Suddenly, Digby the Dinosaur lifted up its head to the sky and let out a long, blood-curdling bellow. As the downtrodden butler released a lifetime of anger and frustration, flocks of Jamaican golden swallows and white-winged sandpipers took flight from the treetops. Below, the ground vibrated under the hooves of blue antelopes, and of unseen herds of stampeding Malagasy dwarf hippopotamuses, as they and every other animal in the forest fled through the undergrowth. But Kruud couldn't escape.

Suddenly the dinosaur's cry stopped and his mighty snout dropped down, level with Kruud's ashen face. As thick, foamy saliva began to drool from the lips of the fellow creature he had taunted for so long, Kruud's eyes bulged with terror knowing that every act of cruelty, every mocking insult, every painful put-down that he had inflicted on his butler was about to be repaid in full. He tried to talk, to beg, to plead, to threaten, but all he could manage were short, panting breaths, each of which pumped him up with more and more fear, until soon his eyes bulged and his skin felt ready to burst. Slowly, the dinosaur's jaws opened to reveal rows of savage, dagger-like teeth, their edges serrated on both sides to create the ultimate shredding machine. Then, as the forest fell silent and the last meringue slipped out of the billionaire's limp hand, Digby lifted Kruud up to his gaping, slavering mouth to take his long-awaited revenge.

'Boo!' he said.

'Aaaaaaaaaaargh!' The word was like a pinprick, releasing the fear inside Kruud so suddenly that he began to deflate like a punctured football. Even worse was the humiliation of being scared almost to death by a tiny, insignificant little 'Boo!' which made him feel so stupid, and small, and pathetic, that he continued to shrivel until soon he was no bigger than a crumb from one of his meringues. Then, with a final look up at the dinosaur, he slipped through its claws and fell – shrinking to nothing before he had a chance to hit the ground.

The moment he had gone Digby's shape began to evolve again, his arms and legs growing thin and bony whilst his fingers spread long and wide, fanning out to support the huge canopies of skin stretched over them, like canvas across the wing frames of Hopper's old biplane. Finally, his snout narrowed and hardened, growing as long as a cricket bat to a sharp, beaky point at the end. Then, as though the chains that had been holding him down for so many years had suddenly been broken, Digby spread his new wings and launched himself off the ground. As he cleared the treetops he soared upwards, lifted by the warm air currents and the sheer delight of having won his freedom. For a few seconds he circled over the tree house, enjoying his complete mastery of the air, before swooping down to land on the roof. With his powerful clawed feet he ripped it open to reveal the mirror standing on the floor inside. He dropped down to perch precariously on top of the wooden frame, flapping his giant wings to remain steady. Then he arched his long neck forward to gaze, upside down, at the reflection of the Grand Fizzler staring back at him from the glass, silent and motionless. The time had come to say goodbye. Slowly, Digby raised his massive prehistoric head skyward before swinging it back down like a demolition ball, his bone-hard beak shattering the glass and sending it to the floor in a thousand crashing pieces. The Grand Fizzler was gone. Once again Digby's mind – and his life – belonged to him.

The television crews looking down from the cliff-top knew nothing of the battle raging inside Digby's mind. Nor did the billions of people watching the Grand Fizzler's speech from the comfort of their living rooms, or huddled around television sets in street cafés, or craning their necks up at the giant screens which had been erected in town squares across the world. They had watched the Grand Fizzler's masterly performance, and listened to his grim warnings of the dangers posed by the Dry-Mouths if they were allowed to remain in their midst. They had seen his eyes grow darker, his brow furrowed, as he described the death and destruction that would follow if action were not taken. This was the Fizzle's message, he claimed, and he conveyed it with a passion and force that few could ignore, and fewer still dared challenge. His followers were mesmerised. The world's people fell silent as his words filled their minds with fear and distrust. The Dry-Mouths were to blame for everything – it made perfect sense. Besides, His Effervescence had told them so often – on television, on the radio, in the newspapers – that it had to be true. As the Grand Fizzler's face darkened and he prepared to make the final announcement for which they had all been waiting, Mr Bloom rose unsteadily from his armchair and, with a shaky hand, bolted his front door. Other Dry-Mouths slipped silently out of the cafés and crowded squares in which they had been watching the speech, or buttoned up their collars to conceal their bare, unpendanted necks. On the Shipley Manor estate, having sent the children early to their dormitories, Roger, Seymour and Edna huddled over a radio, waiting. The dark storm cloud which had been growing around the world was about to burst. And it made the air prickle.

And then . . . the Grand Fizzler had begun to hesitate, lapsing into long, thoughtful pauses as Digby's mind became preoccupied with the battle for control raging inside it. The crowd of onlookers gazing down on the Grand Fizzler had no idea of the struggle for control going on behind his tired old eyes. Digby continued to stare up at them dressed in his Fizzle Finery, his giant illuminated face projected a mile wide so that even aeroplanes flying overhead would have been able to see him clearly. But as Kruud and his associates gradually lost their grip on him he began to falter in mid-sentence, stuttering like an old car that was about to run out of fuel. And now, finally, with Kruud and his associates banished from his mind and the mirror smashed, he had fallen silent.

In the carriage, Pike's face had begun to twitch. Her eyes glued to the television screen above her head, she reached up to increase the volume, giving it a couple of hard slaps on the side for good measure. Why was the old fool hesitating? She scooped the pebbles from the table and began to rattle them together.

'Make him keep to the sssscript, you idiots! Unless all four of you want to end up in a rock grinder!'

But Digby no longer had to play the part of the Grand Fizzler. He no longer had to do or say anything that was demanded of him. Slowly, as the crowds watched, and the television cameras from around the world continued to broadcast his every movement, he removed the crystal pendant from around his neck, and smiled. A murmur spread around the onlookers. Was he about to make a special announcement, as they had all been promised? Indeed he was. But he was in no hurry.

He had waited a long time to reclaim his freedom and he was determined to savour every moment. So, one by one, he began to unpick the glass beads from his beard. Finally, after he had dropped the last one, allowing it to clatter to the floor of the submarine, he gripped the side of his false beard and slowly, inch by inch, peeled it away from his face.

'My name is Digby,' he told them, proudly, 'and I am . . . a Dry-Mouth.'

The world gasped.

Inside the carriage Pike screamed and turned angrily to Polly.

'Did you do this?'

But Polly wasn't there. What was more, the pebbles in Pike's hand felt different, slightly colder than usual. She opened her fist to find four ordinary pebbles from Polly's Jumblupp bag. She turned them over to reveal the letters painted on their reverse sides: I-W-I-N . . . 'I win'.

'We'll ssssee about that,' she snarled, ripping open the hatch and hurling them out into the snow.

'Lukaaaa!'

Super-slug to the Rescue

Polly ran back through the snow, the four pebbles clasped tightly in her hand. As she passed the old shelter she snatched a branch from the roof and began dragging it behind her to disguise her tracks.

Suddenly, just as she heard the sound of snowmobiles approaching in the distance she stopped. She spun around. Trees, and more trees, wave upon wave of snowdrifts – an identical view whichever way she looked, merging into a blurry sameness as she searched for the familiar markers of broken twigs and torn bark, which she'd left to guide her back. She was sure the new shelter was somewhere close, but had no idea in which direction to take her next step. She was lost. Suddenly a hand grabbed her ankle. 'Aaaargh!'

'Quick, get inside,' said Scarlett. Polly dropped to her hands and knees. The shelter had been under her nose the whole time. She wiggled through the narrow gap into the hideout. Then Scarlett piled snow in front of the entrance to seal herself and Polly in.

'We're invisible in here, Polly,' she whispered. 'All we have to do is keep perfectly still and not make a sound.' Polly squeezed Scarlett's hand to show that she understood. The sound of snowmobiles grew louder as the distinctive square prints left by Polly's makeshift snowshoes led them directly to the old shelter. There, the engines stopped. Polly hoped that with no trail left to follow the snowmobiles would head away. Instead, after a few moments, they roared back to life, speeding towards them until the noise outside became deafening. Then they fell silent again. Polly screwed her eyes up tight. She wanted to call secretly for Tom, to tell him where they were so that he and the Captain would race to the rescue. But she knew she couldn't. Pike would overhear her and find them first. Perhaps she already had. Footsteps approached, slow and deliberate, growing louder with each menacing crunch. In the background a voice, muffled by the snow, guided them towards their target.

'Left a bit, right a bit . . . Just there.'

Scarlett held Polly tightly, her hand clamped over her mouth as Polly's teeth began to chatter in the cold. They hadn't been found yet. Keep still. Stay silent. There was still hope.

Suddenly, two pairs of hands began digging frantically through the snow.

'Polly, are you in there? *Polly!*'

Polly recognised the voice. She punched her fist through the snow blocking her in and peered through the narrow hole. A pair of beady brown eyes stared back at her.

'Captain!' She squeezed out of the hideout and threw herself into the Captain's arms. Then she hugged Slugbucket, who had sunk to his knees, tears rolling down his face.

'Yer looked loik you was in a grave, Polly,' he sobbed. 'I thought you was dead!'

Behind them stood Tom, staring down in disgust at the slimy super-slug resting in the palm of his hand.

'You were invisible, Polly,' he said. 'We'd never have found you without Seymour's Slug-o-meter.'

Gingerly, he picked it up and returned it to its matchbox, before pulling a clean handkerchief from his pocket and wiping his hands.

Moolah had already dug Scarlett out of the shelter and wrapped her in a blanket. Then, despite Scarlett's protests that she was quite capable of walking, she had carried her to the caravan. Suddenly the sound of more snowmobiles began echoing through the trees. Polly turned to the Captain.

'They're after my special pebbles,' she told him. 'We have to get away.'

'Polly, this is no time to start worrying about a few old –'

'Look!' she said, displaying them proudly. 'I told you I wasn't imagining them. They're not ordinary pebbles, you see, they're –'

But she couldn't continue. Pike was hurtling through the trees towards them, her golden carriage pulled by six snowmobiles whilst four more, led by Luka, raced ahead. Moolah was already revving her engine. Tom jumped on to his machine and with the Captain, Polly and Slugbucket riding on the steps, and Scarlett cocooned in blankets inside, they sped off.

Had they happened to be racing across open ground the bamboo-masters would have caught them far sooner. Loaded with passengers and with only two snowmobiles to drag it through the snow, the heavy wooden caravan could never hope to outrun Pike's streamlined carriage. But weaving through the trees relied more on skill than speed and Moolah's cat-like reflexes, together with Tom's ability to twist and turn his vehicle as though it were a World War One fighter plane, kept the golden carriage at bay. Suddenly there was a loud explosion behind them. Polly dived back inside the caravan to find Scarlett propped up by the rear window, a smoking flare gun in her hand.

'What would a lifeboat be without a few distress flares, eh?' she said, pointing to the caravan's survival kit lying open at her feet. 'Don't worry, I'm not aiming at the riders, but a few tons of falling snow should slow them down a bit. Pass me another flare, would you?' she said.

Polly handed a flare to Scarlett, then stepped back with her fingers pressed firmly in her ears. There was another bang. Polly raced back to the window and watched with Scarlett as the bright orange flare arced upwards, exploding into the top of a snow-laden pine tree. Suddenly, an avalanche of snow fell into the path of a pursuing snowmobile, which ploughed into it at full speed. Scarlett winked at her new assistant.

'Keep 'em coming, Polly.'

As Polly handed Scarlett flare after flare so the sky filled with ribbons of flaming colour and falling snow. Some of the snowfalls landed directly on top of the pursuing bamboo-masters, others were forced to slow down or change course to avoid colliding with them. But two of Pike's advance riders could not be stopped. No matter how much snow fell in their path they managed either to swerve around it or quickly dig themselves out, remounting their machines to continue their pursuit. Finally, Scarlett loaded the last flare. She waited until the two riders were close together, then fired it into the top of a tree standing directly in their path. Moments later, a ton of snow dropped from its branches to land like a mini-mountain in front of them. For a second or two they could neither be seen nor heard. Then, suddenly, they reappeared, their engines roaring as they flashed either side of the snowfall. Now, there was little more Polly or Scarlett could do but hang on and watch from the window as, with no load to pull, Luka and the other surviving bamboo-master continued to close the gap. Then, as Pike's head appeared out of the carriage behind them, their tactics became clear.

'Force them out of the woods,' she barked. 'Get them out into the open.'

Luka responded, accelerating to draw level with Moolah. As trees flashed past them on either side he stared at her coldly, before steering his vehicle in front of hers, forcing her into the path of an oncoming tree. Moolah turned sharply and Tom with her, both of them passing on one side of the tree whilst Luka veered off on the other. But in avoiding a collision the caravan had moved closer to the edge of the trees. Now they could see open ground through the tree trunks to their left. One more nudge and they would be out of the woods. Again Luka caught up with them and drew alongside Moolah. This time he rammed her, sparks flying up from their blades as the two snowmobiles locked together. Moolah leant to her left, and Tom with her. At the same time she kicked Luka away, separating the two machines just as a huge tree trunk sliced between them. Suddenly, the caravan was out in the open, speeding around the outside of the cliff with nothing but clear snow ahead of it. With the cliff edge looming frighteningly close to them on one side, Tom and Moolah tried to steer back towards the woods. But Luka blocked their path, riding alongside Moolah and resisting every attempt of hers to push him out of the way. Then Pike's carriage broke out of the trees. As the six snowmobiles pulling it accelerated sharply, it began to chase the caravan around the cliff edge as though they were two Roman chariots racing round an arena. With its extra pulling power the carriage caught up quickly, drawing alongside the caravan to push the Captain and his shipmates closer and closer to the cliff edge. As the television crews on the other side of the lake spotted them and turned their cameras – and their powerful spotlights – to follow the chase as it hurtled towards them, Pike leaned out of the carriage.

'Give me back those pebbles, you little brat,' she

screamed.

Suddenly Polly emerged from inside the caravan with four pebbles clasped in her hand. She looked down at the cliff edge just as a wheel clipped one of the 'Keep Out' signs, sending it spinning into the abyss. Any second now and the caravan would follow it. She had to do something.

'If you want the pebbles so much you can have them,' she yelled, finally. 'Catch!'

She threw the four pebbles towards Luka. He steered away from Moolah, reaching up with one hand to grab them. He caught one, then twisted round for another, failing to see another of the signs that he had himself hammered firmly into the snow just two days before. His snowmobile slammed into the post and stopped dead. As he somersaulted through the air Tom and Moolah sped on, whilst the blue riders behind Luka swerved to avoid him, turning sharply to the right. Sadly for Pike, whilst the floats supporting the carriage followed them, the carriage did not. Like a volley of rifle fire the four brackets holding it to the floats snapped in half and, as the two footmen riding on the back jumped clear, the golden droplet, with Pike inside it, sailed in a majestic, graceful arc over the edge of the cliff.

The Golden Teardrop

Every camera tilted forward to watch the carriage as it plummeted like a golden teardrop towards the huge, smiling face of Digby – the self-proclaimed Dry-Mouth – beaming up at the world from the ice a thousand feet below. For a moment he acquired a dimple in his proud, newly revealed chin as the carriage smashed through the ice, sending a huge plume of Fizzle cascading into the air. Immediately, cracks began to spread outwards from the hole, each new fracture echoing around the cliff sides like a crackle of thunder. Then, the surface of the lake began to disintegrate – much like the attic mirror before it – and, for the second time, Digby's face broke into a thousand pieces.

Below it the carriage, its bottom flattened by the impact, continued to sink like a diving bell. With Fizzle gushing in through its portholes – all of which had shattered on impact – Pike prised herself out of the luxury seat in whose deep protective padding she had become firmly wedged. Then, as the Fizzle reached her neck she took a deep breath and swam out through the hatch, leaving the carriage to disappear into the darkness. Immediately, billions of tiny Fizzle bubbles clung to her body to protect her from the icy cold. And then, just as Scarlett and Tom had done before her, she wished for rescue. Once again the Pixelfish responded, taking the form she most desired would lift her out of the icy depth and to safety.

Above, the bamboo-masters having abandoned the chase, Tom and Moolah brought the caravan to a halt and the Shipley Manor crew ran to the cliff edge. As they peered solemnly into the abyss, pondering their pursuer's fate, the head of an enormous snake rose from it as if emerging from a snake-charmer's basket. But this was no ordinary snake. As long and wide as a train, its glowing ruby-red skin was encrusted with precious stones, its belly a swirl of green emeralds, its sides studded with blue sapphires woven into ornate geometric patterns whilst, down its back, a row of diamonds the size of a dustbin lid sparkled under the numerous spotlights which had been trained upon it. And riding on the head of this giant, diamond-backed rattlesnake, her razor-sharp fingernails embedded deep into its skin, was Venetia Pike.

As it reared above the cliff she looked at the world's television cameras directed towards her, then down at Polly and Tom and the other shipmates standing close by. For a few moments Pike looked as shocked as they were. Then, suddenly, everything made perfect sense to her, like the final piece of a jigsaw slotting into place. Of course! This was how it was always meant to be. She was the One. The *real* Grand Fizzler. She was sitting on the proof – a giant jewel-encrusted rattlesnake grander than a thousand royal thrones, created on her instruction and bending to her will like the servant she knew it now to be. Everything she had ever believed about being in charge was true. The Fizzle, and with it the world, was indeed hers to command. She began to cackle with laughter, turning the snake's head from side to side so that everyone could witness her mastery over it. Then she lifted it above Polly and her shipmates.

'They're all Dry-Mouths, too,' she shrieked, pointing a talon at them accusingly, 'just like that impostor in the lake. As you can see beyond any doubt, *I* am the true Grand Fizzler. And it is *I* who will help you rid the world of these filthy maggots once and for all.' She dug her stiletto heels deep into the snake's head, so that it swung down to within a few inches of Polly's terrified face.

'Sssstarting with you,' she said, before hissing to the snake. 'Sssswallow her whole!'

Suddenly there was a flash of steel as the Captain drew out his sword. He stepped in front of Polly, and thrust it forward, holding it firm and steady in front of the snake's huge mouth. If the snake wanted to swallow Polly, it would have to taste his blade first. But the snake didn't strike. Instead, even though the Captain's sword posed no greater threat to it than a plastic toothpick, it retreated, lifting its head to sway gently in front of the world's cameras.

'I command you,' Pike screamed, digging her heels deeper into its flesh. When it ignored her again she began clawing at it, her fingernails clogging up with Pixelfish as she gouged blood-red furrows across its ruby skin.

'Do as I ssssay! Kill her, kill them all!'

But still the Pixelfish did not obey her. Their job was not to kill people. It was to unite them. So, as Pike's rage continued unabated, the snake began slowly to sink back into the Fizzle, dissolving as it went. At the same time, as Pike's screaming, hate-filled descent into the water was watched by billions of people around the world, so their faith in the Fizzle dissolved with it. They had seen enough. The Fizzle hadn't joined people together. With the help of the Grand Fizzler it had brought nothing but division and conflict. They would be better off without it. United behind this single, shared thought, in every living room, in every café, in every village hall and town square where people had gathered to watch the Grand Fizzler's great announcement, his followers began to remove their pendants and drop them to the ground. As the earth echoed to the sound of falling crystal, the Pixelfish knew that today, finally, after thousands of years only one thing remained for them to do, and the task for which they had been created would be complete.

So, as the snake's head, with Pike still clinging to it, disappeared below its surface . . . the lake began to hiss.

Avalanche!

The Fizzle's departure started slowly. The Pixelfish had waited thousands of years for this day and they weren't about to rush it. As Polly and Tom and their shipmates continued to watch from the cliff top, the centre of the lake began to brighten, as though all the glittering Pixelfish were gathering in the centre. Then the Fizzle started to bubble and froth and churn as the billions of tiny creatures in its midst twisted and turned to weave themselves into a single interlocking shape. Suddenly, a gigantic white whale erupted out of the lake, rising hundreds of feet into the air before pirouetting once, twice, and crashing head first back into the water. Having announced its presence it streaked to the outside of the lake where it began to circle, rising and falling in the water as it built up speed, carrying the Fizzle round and round with it in an ever-increasing swirl which began pushing against the cliff walls. Then the whale's body appeared to split apart as the Pixelfish divided themselves into a vast school of swordfish, whose streamlined noses cut even faster through the water. As their tails gradually took the shape of propellers to speed them faster still, so the Fizzle pressed harder and higher against the cliff walls, creating a whirlpool in the middle of the lake wide and deep enough to devour an ocean liner in one gulp.

But the Pixelfish had only just begun. Gradually, the circling swordfish separated into three groups, fanning out from a single point in the centre. As they continued to circle faster and faster, so each swordfish moved closer to its neighbour until, finally, they merged together to become the three solid blades of a single enormous propeller. For a moment it faltered, coughing and spluttering, until – like the engine on Hopper Hawkins's biplane – it exploded into life, the tips of its blades almost scraping the cliff walls as it roared around them in a ghostly blur. Then, it began to rise, pushing ice-cold air up in front of it to tear at the faces of the onlookers on the cliff top, whilst behind it, the force of its half-mile-long blades began slowly to suck the Fizzle out of its ancient home in a massive, spinning waterspout. Halfway up the cliff face the Pixelfish changed shape again, spreading out so that the three propeller blades became hundreds, and the roar became an ear-splitting scream. The Pixelfish had entered the jet age. As the mighty engine continued to suck the Fizzle upwards, the Captain gripped the peak of his cap and turned to his shipmates.

'Time to leave, shipmates,' he shouted, jabbing his finger towards the caravan. 'Quickly now.'

Moments later, Tom and Moolah's snowmobiles were zigzagging through the woods, the caravan jolting unsteadily behind them as the Captain and Slugbucket struggled to keep it upright. Above them, the evening sky filled with the criss-crossing lights of fleeing helicopters, strangely silent, the sound of their blades muffled by the deafening howl of the giant Pixelfish jet engine as it rose closer and closer to the cliff edge. Aboard the helicopters the television crews, their cameras abandoned, clung on as, overloaded with bamboo-masters clinging like stowaways to the undercarriage, the pilots fought to deliver their passengers safely back to the numerous support ships sparkling on the horizon.

As the caravan left the woods, a sudden blast of air pushed it forward. Slugbucket looked back to discover that the huge swirling waterspout had left the confines of the cliff walls and begun spiralling into the sky.

'Now that's what oi calls risin' damp,' he muttered to himself.

He tapped the Captain on his shoulder. 'Yer know,' he bellowed, 'oi reckons the Fizzle kept us frozen on the yacht jus' long enough to make sure we couldn't stop whatsisname's speech. 'Cause if we 'ad done none of this would be 'appenin', would it? This must be what the Fizzle 'ad planned all along.'

The Captain nodded in agreement, just as the two of them leaned sharp left, then right, as Tom and Moolah sped the caravan through a tight cluster of rocks.

'Steady as she goes, shipmates!' he called out to them.

But 'steady' wasn't going to be enough.

As the Pixelfish evolved into ever-faster spinning machines the waterspout had begun to spread outwards, casting a silvery light around it as it sucked at the ground, pulling anything that wasn't fixed down into its hollow, ravenous embrace. Polly threw open the back window of the caravan and looked up into the sky to see snowmobiles, loose rocks and boulders and long, swirling ribbons of snow being sucked up into its heart. And then, heard faintly above the din, the sound of trees creaking as their roots fought in vain to keep them anchored to the ground. One by one, then row by row, they were hoisted out of the frozen earth in a circle of devastation that spread out from the cliff face and began to chase them.

Polly ran to the front of the caravan.

'We have to go faster, it's catching up!'

Tom and Moolah revved the engines as the land began to rise steeply towards the gap in the mountains. From there it was a long ride down the slope to the sea. As they neared the crest of the hill progress slowed. And then, finally, it stopped. Tom's snowmobile, unable to pull the weight of the caravan any longer, had spluttered to a halt, smoke billowing from its motor. The Captain jumped down. He looked back at the woods gradually being consumed behind them. There was only one way to reach Shipley Manor before the waterspout reached them.

'Tom, Moolah, unclip the runner blades from those machines.'

'Polly, put the brakes on the caravan wheels.'

'Slugbucket. Get ready to lift!'

As Polly raced round pressing the brake levers into each wheel rim, the Captain and Slugbucket lifted one side of the caravan out of the snow.

'Ready!'

Tom and Moolah, having removed the two ski-like runners from the first snowmobile, slid one under each raised wheel and clipped it into place.

Then the Captain and Slugbucket let the caravan down and moved quickly to the other side.

'Next!'

In a few seconds the caravan was sitting on four sleek runner blades.

'Now let's get it to the top, shipmates. Ready, steady . . .'

Each crewmate took hold of a wheel and began to push. Quickly, Tom strapped on his snowshoes for extra grip and began pushing the caravan from behind. As they reached the top of the slope the Captain ordered everyone aboard.

'And you, Tom – I'll tip us over.'

'I have to do it, Captain – you're sinking knee deep in the snow. I'm the only one who can give us a really good push off. Besides, I'm small enough to climb in through the back window when we get going.'

The Captain looked up at the waterspout. It was almost overhead. He nodded, and climbed aboard.

'Hold on tight, shipmates,' he bellowed.

Then Tom began to push. As his snowshoes pressed into the snow the caravan moved, gradually picking up speed as it began its descent, one metre, two, four, eight, feeling lighter and lighter as it slid under its own weight. Suddenly, Tom was no longer pushing – he was trying to catch up as the smooth runners, and the weight of the Shipley Manor crew, propelled it faster and faster towards the sea. Slugbucket reached out his hand, then Polly stretched out with her Fizzlestick, but Tom was beyond reach of either of them. Finally, Slugbucket threw out a length of rope.

'Catch!'

Tom managed to pick up the trailing end just before it tightened, jolting him forward. He managed to stay upright and tried to run, but he could feel the caravan pulling him forward. Any moment his feet would get left behind and he would topple over. He needed to lean back. He needed to ski. The skills Hopper Hawkins had learned on the skiing slopes of the Rocky Mountains were something Tom had expected only ever to use on holiday. Now he found himself skiing for his life. As the caravan sped down the mountain he clung on, keeping his knees bent to absorb the bumps and his heels pressed down so that the forward edges of the flat 'Keep Out' signs on which he was skiing didn't dip into the snow and send him cartwheeling down the slope. Behind him, the waterspout had clipped the top of the mountain and, as he glanced backwards, he knew that the rumble that followed could mean only one thing. An avalanche.

A huge, roaring wave of snow and ice had begun to slide down the mountain towards them. And it was travelling faster than they were. On the caravan steps the Captain tried to keep their course straight and steady, leaning left or right whenever the caravan seemed to be veering to either side. Each time, Tom adjusted his course to match, dipping a knee and ankle inward to send curtains of snow flying into the air either side of him. But each swerve slowed them down. Tom glanced back at the massive white wall thundering after him, blocking out his view of the mountain from which it had come.

Suddenly the Captain bellowed over his shoulder.

'Rocks, Tom. Look out!'

Having spotted them just moments before, the Captain had known there was little chance of avoiding them. All he could do was steer straight over them and warn Tom. No sooner had the Captain called to him than Tom saw a group of snow-covered boulders – lying together like a family of curled up polar bears – appear between the wheels of the caravan. Whilst the caravan itself was high enough to clear them, the small red outboard motor attached to its rear was not. The rocks smashed into it, ripping it instantly from its mounting. As a piece of broken propeller blade whistled past Tom's ear he dug his right heel into the snow and veered wide to avoid the obstruction whilst the motor flew past him, embedding itself like a clown's nose in the face of the advancing snow.

Now the avalanche roaring after him had begun spitting snow at his heels, like white froth pushed ahead of a breaking wave. Slugbucket could see that it would soon catch him.

'Steady yerself, Tom, I'm pullin' you in.'

Hand over hand, as the Captain did his best to keep the caravan steady, Slugbucket began to pull the rope in, drawing Tom closer and closer to the back of the caravan.

'Hang on, Tom, we nearly got yer.'

Suddenly a huge arm reached out of the window and grabbed him, lifting him off the ground and pulling him against the back of the caravan. Then more hands reached out as Polly and Moolah helped Slugbucket haul him inside. As Tom tumbled through the opening, his snowshoes snapped off against the window frame, spinning wildly before landing edge first in the snow like crooked gravestones, only to be buried themselves a split second later.

Then, as the avalanche began to snap at the caravan's wheels they approached the shoreline. The Captain steadied their course as the land dipped sharply to meet the ice, and prepared to fire them out across the ocean.

'Hang on, shipmates, here we goooooo . . .'

As the caravan became airborne the four runner blades, detached from their weighty burden, launched themselves like missiles across the ice sheet. The caravan landed a split second behind them, spinning across the ice pursued by the avalanche, which continued to push out into the ocean like a huge white tongue. As the edge of the ice sheet came into view the snow caught up with them, nudging them along the last few metres before tipping them into the water. There the wall of snow stopped, teetering over them like a reluctant swimmer too scared to take the plunge. But the danger had not passed. Ahead, a network of water channels lay between them and Shipley Manor. With water now up to the top of the caravan's wheels the creaks and cracks that Polly had heard during their descent took on a greater meaning. Water had begun seeping into the caravan through splits in the wood.

The Captain ducked inside to pull a pair of paddles from under the bunk.

'The waterspout's spreading this way,' he told them. 'We need to get on board Shipley Manor as quickly as possible. Slugbucket and I will start paddling. Polly, you've always been good at mazes – come to the front and find us the quickest route through all these channels.' He looked down at the freezing water that was covering the floor like a shallow puddle. 'The rest of you will have to find whatever you can to bail out that water. Keep us afloat, shipmates.'

A few seconds later Polly stood between the two paddlers, scanning the ice sheets and the channels of water which ran between them. As the bow of Kruud's yacht came into view on the other side of the peninsula, the Captain reached inside his coat and pulled out his telescope. He handed it to Polly and continued paddling.

'Can you see Mr Grub, Polly?'

'No. But I can see a submarine,' she replied. 'It's just come to the surface alongside the yacht. There's something pink and furry stuck to the glass bubble on top. I think it's moving.'

Then Polly watched as, half a mile away, Pike peeled herself from the top of the submarine, her fur coat as dry as a bone, and climbed on to the narrow gangplank leading into its side. Although Polly couldn't hear Pike's voice, she could sense her rage as Digby refused to follow her. Then, as the submarine sank slowly beneath the waves, Pike turned and looked straight towards the caravan, before charging up the gangplank into the yacht.

As the freezing wind whistled around their ears, Slugbucket and the Captain continued to paddle through the choppy water channels. Polly glanced back at her shipmates, desperately hurling water out of the back window in an effort to keep the caravan from sinking. Then she looked up at the sky. She had always believed that anything was possible. But now, in front of her eyes, the Pixelfish were proving it. Connected not just to every great scientist and engineer who had drunk the Fizzle on Fizzle Friday, but to every other living thing which had absorbed it as it seeped back into the earth, they were combining the genius of both to reshape themselves. As they continued to create machines of such complexity that no single mind, not even the greatest of nations, could do more than dream about them, the Pixelfish drew the glittering silver waterspout ever higher into the sky, spreading it wide and flat in a hypnotic display of power that caused Polly's mouth to drop open.

Suddenly, the wind whipped a strand of frosty hair across her face and reminded her that she had a job to do. She snapped her attention back to the ice, looking for ways through the zigzag of water channels which lay between them and Shipley Manor. They were almost there.

'Take the next channel on the left, Captain,' she shouted. 'That will take us straight to the house.'

The Captain nodded.

'Any sign of Mr Grub yet?' he yelled.

Polly lifted the telescope to her eye. How strange

. . . the yacht was gone. Then, as she lowered it again, she understood why. Kruud's yacht was on the move – tearing through the semi-darkness at full speed, its sharp, angular bow ripping the sea ice apart as though it were nothing more than damp tissue . . .

. . . and it was heading straight for Shipley Manor.

The Rattler's Revenge

The Captain and his crew could do nothing but watch as Pike drove the yacht hard into the back of Shipley Manor. She aimed it directly between the paddle wheels, so that the pointed bow drove straight through the raised drawbridge and deep into the old oak doors behind it. They exploded into a thousand splinters before what was left was ripped off its hinges as the yacht's bow crashed through into the courtyard. The impact sent the drawers in Polly's cabin leaping out of her bedside cabinet, every plate, cup and saucer in the kitchen flying off its shelf, every one of the Captain's ancestors spinning to the floor as their portraits jumped out of their picture hooks. In the cargo hold aboard Kruud's yacht a thousand crates smashed open, their deadly contents spilling out over the floor like the abandoned weapons of two enormous armies. In the ballroom, Pike's huge money mountain toppled forward, demolishing the Grand Fizzler's television studio in a clinking, clanking avalanche that spilled far out into the corridor. Further along in the yacht's control room, Barclay Grub came tumbling out of his hiding place, to land at Venetia Pike's feet.

She didn't turn. Distracted by the sound of exploding wood and of the Arctic Ocean flooding in to fill the courtyard, she stepped out of the door and on to the balcony in front of the control room. There, she looked across at Polly and the Captain standing ashen-faced and silent on the steps of Slugbucket's caravan, watching as the great house, home to the Captain's family for over two centuries, began slowly to sink into the water. Pike yelled at them across the ice, her face twitching with pleasure, her claw-like hands raised in triumph.

'I win! . . . *I win!*'

With one last delicious look at the water surging through Shipley Manor's shattered entrance, Pike realised that the time had come to reverse the engines and allow the Arctic Ocean to complete her work. She turned to find Barclay Grub standing behind her, his sweaty hands clamped together in excitement. Then, trembling with joy, he threw his arms around her and hugged her tight.

'Venetia!'

'Let me go, you little worm,' Pike shrieked, trying to wriggle free. 'What are you doing here? Why aren't you rotting in jail where you belong? Get away from me!'

But Grub was deaf to her protests. His beloved Venetia – his darling fluffy bunny – was alive, and all he could hear was the sound of his heart pounding with joy. Suddenly the yacht lurched as Shipley Manor, its courtyard already half full of swirling, ice-cold water, tilted forward.

'We have to get out of here,' Pike screamed at him ferociously. 'The house is going to sink. Barclay! *Barclay!*'

Still he clung on, his eyes shut tight in ecstasy, the events unfolding in the sky above him now drowning out all other sound. Pike looked up to find that the whirling, spinning waterspout had grown several miles wide and, even though it was no longer connected to the ground and was rising fast, its pull on the air around them seemed only to be increasing. And it had begun to glow. But the Fizzle couldn't leave any part of itself behind. All of it was connected. So it began to gather itself together, withdrawing from every living thing in preparation for its final journey.

Tom felt it straightaway. Like his shipmates, and the billions of other people around the world who had drunk the Fizzle, he felt a sudden tingling in his toes. Gradually it moved up his body, growing into a hot prickly feeling which made his cheeks blush as though he'd been caught eating the last slice of chocolate cake. And then he could feel it tickling his scalp. For a moment he lifted himself on to his toes as if to delay the moment when the Fizzle would finally leave him. It had been part of him for so long, saved his life and seen him through so many adventures that, for a moment, he didn't want it to go. But he knew it must. So he let it leave, feeling it rise like a shiver from the top of his head. He looked up to see a faint, silvery wisp curling upwards like steam from a cup of hot tea. Then it accelerated, drawing a luminous trail through the darkness as it streaked upwards to join the ever-growing waterspout. A moment later it was gone and, to his surprise, Tom felt free. But not alone. As the world shivered, so the night sky lit up as billions of other light trails, like silver threads woven into an enormous tapestry, flashed across the sky to join the glittering swirl. As it grew, so the Pixelfish sped faster still, drawing the Fizzle together from even the farthest corners of the earth.

Below, around Shipley Manor, the ice-cold air whistled and howled with increasing ferocity, and Polly and her shipmates stared in horror as the old stone house, their home, continued to sink slowly into the ocean. There was nothing they could do. Tears frozen like salty icicles to their cheeks, oblivious to the storm raging around them or the Fizzle commandeering the sky above, they watched the water creep up the ancient walls and, one by one, said their silent goodbyes.

Suddenly, Polly spotted a flash of white inside the Crow's Nest.

'Nautipus!'

She lurched forward.

'Oh no, you don't,' cried Slugbucket, holding her back. He looked at the short stretch of ice between the caravan and what remained of the house. ''E's my cat – I'll get 'im.'

'And he's a member of my crew,' the Captain yelled into the wind, 'and I'm not about to abandon a shipmate, not even a white fluffy one.'

But it was Moolah who won the argument, pushing past both of them and leaping on to the ice, landing as sure-footedly as the cat she was determined to save.

'And I'm the quickest!' she called back over her shoulder as she raced towards the house. Little of it remained above the surface now. Huge, sickening bubbles had begun gurgling around it as the walls slid deeper and deeper into the ocean. At the edge of the ice she leaped up, reaching for the low wall which ran around the outside of the roof. She grabbed it and hoisted herself up, rolling over it on to the roof just as water began to spill through its stone balustrading.

By the time she had reached the inner wall overlooking the courtyard she was knee deep in icy water. Rising above her, one more jump away, was the Crow's Nest, the tower below cracked where the bow of Kruud's yacht had smashed through the doors and kept on going. The bow was still there, pressed against the tower like an arrow striking its target. Further back, on the balcony outside the control room, she could see Pike. Pressed against the railings she was wrestling to free herself from Grub's embrace as the yacht – tilting forward so steeply that its propellers stuck out of the water – threatened to follow Shipley Manor into the ocean.

Moolah jumped up on to the wall, stumbling clumsily as her legs, numbed by the icy water, failed to do as they were told. She rubbed them hard and prepared to leap over to the Crow's Nest. From there, once she had Nautipus tucked safely under her coat, she would drop down on to the yacht and rescue Mr Grub – not that he appeared to want rescuing. As the water once again reached her feet she crouched low, then launched herself upwards and out over the water. She managed to catch the bottom of the railings which ran around the Crow's Nest balcony, heaving herself up the ironwork and over on to her feet. She burst into the Crow's Nest just as every window on the ground floor caved in.

Suddenly, water exploded into the house, filling the kitchen and the Captain's cabin, and rising up through the building to drag it down. As Shipley Manor lurched forward a wall of water surged against the Crow's Nest, forcing the door shut. With the Crow's Nest slipping slowly into the darkness, Moolah pounded, then kicked, then charged at the door trying to open it again. But the weight of water pressed against it was too great. As she picked up a chair and began hammering it in vain against the safety glass, her last sight was of the Captain's cap flying off in the wind, as he and Slugbucket raced across the ice towards her.

And then she was gone. The Captain threw off his heavy coat and dived after her, his cheeks puffed out like huge, frosty tomatoes. As the cold pierced his body like a thousand icicles thrust deep into his skin he fought to open the door. But it wouldn't budge. Moolah was trapped, and no amount of hammering on the window, from outside or in, would smash the safety glass. Now only Kruud's yacht – wedged tight between the courtyard's inner walls – was keeping Shipley Manor, and her with it, from sinking to the bottom. Exhausted and with no Fizzle to warm him the Captain kicked up to the surface, numb with cold and shaking uncontrollably. Far above him he could hear Pike screaming at Grub as the wind howled around them and the yacht on which they stood sank deeper and deeper into the ocean. Suddenly Slugbucket's huge hands dragged the Captain out of the water and slung him over his shoulders like a soggy rolled-up carpet. He carried him to the caravan and laid him on the bunk inside. Polly threw down her bailing bucket.

'Captain!'

'Pile as many blankets on 'im as you can, Polly, then rub 'is 'ands an' feet ter warm 'im up. I'm goin' back for Moolah. Scarlett an' Tom, you keep bailin' – this caravan's all we got now.'

He turned to leave, but at that moment the barrel-shaped roof of the caravan was ripped off and sucked into the sky, twisting and turning as though it were no heavier than a paper bag. There it joined the thousands of trees that had been uprooted from the mountainsides as the Fizzle grew and expanded to fill the entire sky. Tom looked around at the sea, rough and rippling in the channels between the ice sheets which were appearing to bend upwards under the magnetic pull of the vacuum at the heart of the waterspout. Suddenly the blankets covering the Captain were whipped out of his grip and lifted skyward. Tom realised that this time, no matter how much he wished it, no matter how much he believed that anything was possible, the Fizzle wouldn't be able to save them. The world had wanted it to leave, and it was granting that wish in the only way it could.

As the wind turned from a howl to a scream, Slugbucket dragged his shipmates to the floor and threw himself across them, hoping to keep them safe under his weight. Pressing his hands and feet hard against the walls of the caravan, he wedged himself tight, wishing he was heavier, or made of stone – or anything that would stop him and his shipmates from following the roof up into the sky. He closed his eyes and hung on, feeling the air tug at the back of his jacket like an army of invisible hands. Next, he felt a shudder and, slowly but unmistakably, the caravan, and he and his shipmates along with it, parted company with the ocean and rose into the air. Then, suddenly, it stopped. Slugbucket opened his eyes. Sure enough, the caravan had risen out of the water, and the air was still trying to suck the old brown coat from his back. But they weren't suspended in mid-air as he had expected. Instead, a voice was calling to him.

'Can I be of any assistance, sir?'

Slugbucket looked down at the submarine which had risen beneath them and on which the caravan – or what was left of it – now rested. Then he caught sight of Digby's head poking out from a nearby hatchway like a tortoise peering out from its shell.

'Hurry, sir!' the butler shouted, beckoning him aboard. 'I fear we don't have much time.'

Together at Last

As the submarine carried the Captain and his crew beneath the waves, Barclay Grub opened his eyes and gazed up momentarily at the huge, glowing waterspout which had spread high above them. How romantic. He closed them again and breathed in the faint fishy scent of his beloved Venetia. Oblivious to all but his own joy at being reunited with her, he could neither hear her screaming at him, nor feel the hard blows raining down on his back as she fought to free herself from his deadly embrace. But he wouldn't let her go. He had lost her once, and had vowed never to do so again. Her fur hat, followed closely by her white-blonde wig, had long since disappeared into the void, sucked off her head like feathers into a jet engine. And now it was their turn. As the ice around the yacht, whose bow already dipped deep into the water, buckled and cracked and began to rise in a thousand jagged, spinning shards all around them, Pike stopped hitting him. Instead, she clasped the railing behind her back as the air started to suck her and Grub off their feet. Now nothing was holding them down but Pike's talony grip. But she held firm, clinging to life for those last few precious seconds before either the dark ice-cold sea or the huge whirling cataclysm circling overhead sucked her up into the stars. Then, as she felt the icy water rising over her ankles, she let go. As she released her grip on the railings, Grub's hold on his beloved Venetia merely increased. Spiralling up into the heart of the waterspout he hugged her close, his eyes tight shut in the joyful certainty that everything in the universe was finally as it should be, and that the two of them would be together for eternity. As they rose ever faster into the sky, as though transported inside an invisible lift, Pike looked down as, thousands of feet below, Kruud's gleaming white yacht disappeared, along with its evil cargo, beneath the waves.

Below the surface, huddled together inside the submarine's glass observation bubble, Scarlett and the crew of Shipley Manor scanned the dark waters for any sign of the house. Suddenly, in the distance some way below them, Polly spotted a faint light swinging from side to side.

'Moolah's still alive, look!' she said. 'She's signalling from the Crow's Nest with a torch.'

Suddenly the submarine lurched forward as Digby caught sight of the former bamboo-master peering out from behind the glass. She had been one of his worst tormentors – her face one that he would never forget.

The Captain, still shivering beneath a layer of blankets, called down to him in the steering room.

'Steady as she g-g-g-goes, old chap.'

But Digby appeared not to hear. Instead, the submarine began to travel towards the Crow's Nest at collision speed. Behind the glass, Moolah's eyes widened as the submarine tore through the darkness towards her. She waved the oncoming submarine aside, but it seemed to speed faster and faster. Tom jumped down from the observation bubble and tried to open the steering-room door. But it was locked. He hammered on the metal.

'Digby, slow down!'

Then, together, he and Slugbucket tried to force the hatch open.

'Of course,' said Polly, running to join them, 'Moolah says she used to treat Digby even worse than she treated the boys in Mr Kruud's factory.'

'But she ain't loik that no more,' Slugbucket replied. 'She wouldn't 'urt a fly.'

'He doesn't know that. He must have recognised

her and now he wants revenge.' She hammered on the door. 'Digby, can you hear me? *Please stop*!'

But the submarine continued on its course, straight as a torpedo. Moolah switched off the torch, hoping that the submarine might not hit her, but by now the Crow's Nest was under the full glare of its powerful headlights. As the submarine drew closer Moolah spotted Digby's face in the steering-room window. She stepped back from the glass and hugged Nautipus close to her chest as Digby stared back at her, his face menacing and determined in the eerie red glow of the instrument panel. But he had no intention of harming her. As numerous hands continued to pound on the steering-room door, there was a triumphant cry from inside – 'Digby the Daredevil!' – and he pushed the controls forward. The submarine dipped sharply, slamming into the tower with pinpoint accuracy just below the Crow's Nest, opposite the bow of Kruud's yacht which was still embedded in the stonework. Like the Captain and his crew, Digby was thrown forward, smashing his nose against the steering-room window. But the reinforced glass held firm. For a few moments the submarine hung limp in the water, rising slightly so that he was face to face with Moolah. He gestured to her, 'Hold on', then, as huge bubbles exploded from the tower, the crack which Kruud's yacht had made in it ruptured wide open and the Crow's Nest – the biggest air bubble of them all – broke free. As Kruud's yacht and the rest of Shipley Manor faded into the darkness, the Crow's Nest, transformed from coffin to escape pod, floated upwards cocooned in silvery bubbles until, finally, it bobbed to the surface.

His rescue mission accomplished, Digby pulled hard on the controls and brought the flat-nosed but otherwise undamaged submarine up to join it. As the crew of Shipley Manor climbed out into night, they found the air to be still, and the ocean – from which the ice had disappeared for as far as the eye could see – as calm and flat as a village pond. Moolah was waiting for them on the Crow's Nest balcony, the head of a fluffy white cat peeping out from beneath her coat. Moments later Digby emerged from the steering room. As he climbed slowly through the hatch to join them, a crisp white handkerchief pressed over his nose, a seal poked its snout haughtily out of the water to greet him.

'Arf!' it said.

'I agree, Arthur,' replied Digby, tipping his head back. 'I really must get that steering-room lock fixed.'

Then his mouth dropped open.

'Goodness me, look at that,' he said.

Fifty miles above them, shimmering in the

darkness like a galaxy of glittering new stars, the Fizzle had flattened out wide and wafer-thin across the sky, spiralling around a single speck of blackness. Combining the sum of all human knowledge with the genius of nature, this was the Pixelfish's final creation – its form so dense and complex that every Pixelfish in the lake was packed into a space no wider than a tractor tyre. And it was getting smaller, shrinking minute by minute into nothingness, as its pure, irresistible spin drew itself and everything around it towards the all-devouring hole in its centre. From this, like a whirlpool in the night, there came no sound, no colour, no light and no chance of escape. As the Fizzle protected them inside a bubble of cool, clean air, Venetia Pike and Barclay Grub – his arms still wrapped around her in an endless bear hug – continued to rise towards it. By now far beyond reach of the Captain's telescope, Pike looked down. Below them, the curve of the earth stretched in a graceful protective arc over the jagged white contours of the Arctic coast, and the deep-blue ocean from which they had come. Directly above them, drawing them ever closer, was the hole. The Fizzle had begun to flow through it now, like a sheet of liquid silk being pulled through a buttonhole. Where it was going Pike couldn't tell. She could see nothing in the hole, nor anything through it. All she knew was that this time the Fizzle couldn't save her. All it could do was take her on its journey, even though she was no longer part of it. The Fizzle had left her body too, just as it had left every person who had ever drunk it, or breathed in its all-powerful gas. Gone was the ability it had bestowed on her to read other people's thoughts, and to sneak into their minds. Gone were the skills she had stolen from Hopper Hawkins, and her control over Sherman H. Kruud and his pebbly associates. Gone was the unimaginable wealth and power which she had accumulated since Fizzle Friday, along with all ambition, and all hope. She had nothing now. Except Barclay Grub. Sweaty, lovesick, barking mad Barclay Grub. So, as they joined the last of the Fizzle on its journey into oblivion, to Grub's blissful, gurgling delight, she hugged him back.

Voices

Tom closed his eyes and began to count backwards. Suddenly, he could hear Polly's voice as clearly as if she were sitting opposite him.

'Say something then,' she said.

'Like what?'

'I don't know. Pretend you haven't spoken to me since we got back from the Arctic.'

'But that was a year and a half ago.'

'Well, you should have lots of questions then, shouldn't you?'

Tom sighed.

'All right then . . . where are you?'

'In the Slugbus café, with a plateful of chocolate brownies. I've been helping Mum and Edna and the Captain bake millions of them for tomorrow's Grand Opening.'

'Grand Opening of what?'

'The Shipley Manor Academy. The whole town's coming. Mr Tutt and your dad and Slugbucket are draping bunting over the entrance now. I can see Digby and Moolah there too, polishing the special plaque on the wall.'

'What does it say?'

'It says: *In memory of Harry "Hopper" Hawkins.* Scarlett's arriving tomorrow to cut the ribbon.'

'What else can you see?'

Polly bent down to stroke Nautipus, before returning to the window.

'I can see Carlos and Calypso by the lake, feeding Arthur. Seymour's watching them from the Crow's Nest. That's in the middle of the lake now, on top of an even bigger helter-skelter. The Captain says I can be the first one down into the water tomorrow, after the opening.'

'Have you told him what our password was yet?'

'A hundred times. But each time I say, "Guess," he says, "Mmmm, let me see . . ." and starts working his way through the alphabet. Yesterday he did P – pilot, pendant, Pike, parrot, perch, polar bear, pebble. He still hasn't worked it out.'

'Have you checked your "magic" pebbles today?'

Tom heard the sound of rattling as Polly retrieved a K, P, R and C from her Jumblupp bag.

'The lights inside still haven't come back,' she told him. 'I could have let Venetia Pike have them after all.'

'Perhaps Mr Kruud and the others left with the Fizzle, along with our special way of talking to each other.'

'Maybe.'

'Do you miss being able to do that?'

Polly paused, as though she were chewing over the question.

'No. This is better.'

Tom opened his eyes, across the table from her.

'Then why did you want me to pretend we were doing it again?'

Polly started to laugh.

Tom looked down.

'You've eaten all the brownies!'

Cast in order of extinction

Pterodactyl – *c.*65 million years ago
Cave bear – *c.*25,000 years ago
Woolly rhino – *c.*10,000 years ago
Malagasy dwarf hippo – *c.*1,000 years ago
Great elephant bird – 1649
White-winged sandpiper – 1777
Blue antelope – 1799
Black-browed babbler – 1850
Cuban red macaw – 1864
Vietnam warty pig – 1892
Mangarevan whistler – late 19c
Alfaro's hummingbird – *c.*1900
Gypsy moth (in Britain) – 1907
Laughing owl – 1914
Small key mouse – 1920
Paradise parrot – 1927
Desert rat-kangaroo – 1935
Pink-headed duck – 1935
Yellow-billed pintail – 1952
Imperial woodpecker – 1956
Guam flying fox – 1968

Jamaican golden swallow – 1990
Red gazelle – 1994
Black spider monkey – Endangered
Ghost-faced bat – Endangered

Dates of extinction are approximate only

Acknowledgements

Huge thanks go to Jo, Jessica, Sarah and Samuel for their continued inspiration and support during the writing of this book, to Maurice Markson for allowing 'Hopper' Hawkins to borrow his handlebar moustache, and to Julia and all the team at Faber for their hard work and expert guidance over the course of the series.

AT A LOOSE END?

Visit

faberkids

Win stuff – great competitions each month.

Have your say – join the kidszone panel and have your say about your likes, dislikes and what you've been reading.

Play games – visit our microsites and play our addictive games Nut Ding, Manic Mundi and The Parliament of Blood. More coming soon!

More stuff – read extracts from our latest books, listen to audio clips, find out about your favourite authors and much more.

It's all at:
www.faberkids.co.uk

Just read a Faber book? Let us know what you think. Send your review to kidszone@faber.co.uk. Your review might feature on the website and will be entered for our review of the month competition.